ALT-REICH
A LITFPS NOVEL

CRAIG SAUNDERS

SEVERED PRESS
HOBART TASMANIA

ALT-REICH

WWW.SEVEREDPRESS.COM

ISBN: 978-1-925711-44-8

ACKNOWLEDGEMENTS

With special thanks to Ian Woodhead –friend, writer, and moderately nice person.
To Gary Lucas and Severed Press for the opportunity. Writing a book about playing games, you say?! Hell yes.
And as always, to you. Thank you for reading.

Craig
The Shed
2017

PART ONE
OLD SCHOOL

SCORE   HEALTH
0   0001
-
Gauntlet
– Atari Games 1985/ZX Spectrum port Gremlin Graphics Software/1987

CHAPTER ONE

Massachusetts, U.S.A.
2017

There's a point in a man's life - a woman's, too - when they realise they're going to die. Not a distant possibility, but a harsh reality that's utterly inescapable. It doesn't matter what you do, you *are* going to die.

Henry Brandon reached that point in his doctor's office at three fifteen in the afternoon, Middlesex County, MA, as he stared at kid's drawings on a wall cupboard in slanting autumn light. He wasn't really listening to the doctor. He got the gist. He wasn't stupid. Overweight, nudging fifty, unfit and unlikely to get any fitter...all of those. But not stupid.

He was on his way to heart attack county.

At forty-nine years old, it was around a decade after life became a temporary thing, but it was only then, in that crisp, clean room that Henry Brandon truly understood just how finite life was.

He stared at the drawings on the cupboard, didn't listen, and thought about cholesterol and globules and wobbling things which shouldn't rightly wobble.

There were three pictures, drawn on A4 paper. Must've been drawn by the doctor's kids, he figured, because ordinary people didn't keep stranger's kid's drawings in their office.

Below the drawings was a picture of the doctor and his family, probably, on a trip involving bikes and maybe a picnic. Fruit – strawberries, kiwis, dragon fruit. Weird things healthy people ate and doctors could afford.

Henry (never Hank, always Henry) had a fair pot belly, and scrawny arms and legs. He owed a nearly-dead flatbed truck, didn't have a job any longer, used to have a wife who he'd managed to lose somewhere along the way, too. Three kids had all left home, the youngest twenty-five years old. She'd sent him a Christmas card, at least.

This year? Last year?

Henry couldn't really remember, and it didn't matter all that much. Pain and hurt are just as temporary as life.

What did he have left? Disabled, walking with two sticks because of a back that'd ache from now until he died.

"Cholesterol's more than dangerously high, Henry. Anything up over 200 is not cool. You're nudging *300*."

"What are you saying, doc? I'm done?"

"No, Hank. I'm saying you *could* be. Honestly? You *will* be...if you don't do something. Eat a healthier diet. Move around more. Join a gym."

"Gym?" Henry laughed.

He fell quiet for a moment and the doctor didn't say anything, but waited while Henry stared back at the pictures on the wall. Happiness drawn in coloured pencils by the kids of the healthy, wealthy man who rode a bike worth more than Henry's truck.

"I can't move around much, doc. My truck's just about closer to dying than me. I hope. Broke back, broke bank. Most expensive thing I got is my PC and most of that I jury-rigged with bits here, bits there. I got it so I didn't have to go to the grocers, and by now I'm not so sure any of it's what I bought in the first place. When I'm bored, or when the pain's so bad I can't move, I play. I get the games from the thrift store. TV got took last year. They didn't want the damn truck. Believe that? Didn't want the truck. I hid the PC in the shed with the pickles and the lawn mower. I've got Internet, but no cable, no satellite. I wash in cold water."

The doctor, a pretty nice man, all in all, just listened. It didn't really matter if Henry talked for another hour. He was a rare doctor. One who thought treating a patient wasn't just about the ailment, but about the patient.

Henry wasn't a proud man, either. He didn't care if the doctor heard all about the state of his world. He didn't care about an awful lot, right then, and if he was honest, it'd been a long time since he'd cared much about much.

"Fair enough, but you don't need a gym, Henry. A couple of cans for weights. The floor, even. A pair of shoes. Go for a walk..." the doctor thought better of that, 'well, move a couple of cans of peaches around. Eat a little less if you can't afford to eat better. The money you save, spend on something else. Hell, get one of those VR headsets. Wave your arms around on the couch if you have to. Eat less, move more. It's no more complicated than that, and doesn't have to cost anything. In fact, it'll cost you *less*. You're not hugely overweight – it's your diet which is the problem. Henry, I've been your doctor for a long time. All of this is

2

optional, of course. I can give you something to lower the cholesterol, sure...but without making some changes?" The doctor shrugged, and held out his palms. Like, what are you going to do?

"I get it, doctor. I do."

"A man's life isn't mine to change. But advice, Henry? You're getting chest pains. Your weight's making your back worse. You're not moving and not working and I'm concerned about your mood. Choice is this, Henry – change something, or..."

Henry gave the man credit for not giving him a sympathetic smile along with the pep talk.

"OK."

Henry stood.

"Think about it?"

"Already did," said Henry, and shook the doctor's hand.

"You like games, right?"

"Always," said Henry, smiling. Wives, kids, dogs...they came and went. If he still had a PC, he had...*escape*.

"There are no reloads," said the doctor. "Right?"

"Truth," said Henry, and nodded his thanks as he closed the door behind him.

CHAPTER TWO

Galway, Ireland
1970

Field Marshall Hunter sat with a heavy sigh at his desk. A green leather blotter covered most of the writing surface, the rest built of a dark, reddish wood. The whole thing was probably heavy enough to knock down a wall. A large drawer on the right held Scotch - Lagavulin – and two crystal glasses from Waterford. Good crystal wouldn't be coming out of Waterford any longer. This was Eire – all that was left of it. Here, just south from Galway on the west coast, was the last Allied base left on the isle.

German boats filled the bay, and the Nazis owned this last European bastion against the insatiable *Kaiserreich* from Cork to Belfast, and from Dublin all the way to Hunter's command, here, where a man could imagine if he squinted and strained his eyes as the sun set, he might see the Americas out over the ocean.

This is where Europe ends.

It was true...

This is not where we lose, though.

...and that was just as true.

He vowed to remember that as he met his very own bullet.

Hunter pulled the cork and filled his glass to the brim, his hand shaking as he did so. The scotch overflowed and spilled across the desk. He filled the second glass, too. Meeting your death, it seemed like the right thing to do – to offer your killer a drink. Killing a man while you look him in the eye wasn't easy. It shouldn't be.

Hunter waited, looking between his last drink and the door.

A gunshot rang out down the hall, then, a barrage.

Hunter prided himself on a good ear. *MP 34*. Manufactured by the *Waffenfabrik Steyr*. There were newer, better weapons out there, but like his American cousins were so fond of saying - why change it if it ain't broke?

"Hmm...Something like that."

4

The man who came to end the Field Marshall's career, and life, smashed the door open with the heel of a black boot. The door wasn't even locked.

How very uncouth.

But even when faced with rudeness, a gentleman should always remain a gentleman.

"Drink?" said Hunter, indicating the Scotch across from him on the desk.

"The plans," said the man. His accent wasn't German, or Austrian. Not even something Hunter could place as an Axis tone.

"I'm surprised. I thought you'd be more...German."

French? Swiss? Hunter's ear was great with guns, not so good with accents, but he placed it, finally, by ticking through some kind of library of warped vinyl in his mind.

"A *mercenary*? Good heavens," said Hunter. "Afrikaner? That's a turn up for the old books, isn't it?"

The man, broad in the shoulder, but not heavy, was blonde with pale skin and deep set eyes. His eyes were placid. Hunter understood something as the Afrikaner shook his head – this man didn't need a stiff drink to take a life.

"The plans, please, Field Marshall. Let's not drag this out."

"I always thought it would take a certain kind of class to share a drink with one's killer. I must say, I'm having second thoughts."

"We can get this done with no unnecessary mess."

"Doesn't matter at all," said Hunter, and took a healthy dose of Lagavulin to wash the taste of the man in the doorway from his mouth. "The plans are long gone. Your arrival isn't a surprise, man. Nazi boots and tanks stomping across the continent for thirty years? We did notice, you know."

"And you won't tell, will you?" said the man, his warm submachine gun pointing without so much as a tremor at Hunter's chest.

"Under duress? Of course I would. But you believe me, don't you? Because if I did know, or if the plans were sitting here in my drawer, I wouldn't be sitting drinking Scotch, waiting for you to bloody well get on with it, would I?"

"Very reasonable. Very...British."

Hunter took that as a compliment, whether intended or not.

"And Herr Professor Sauer whereabouts, Field Marshall? Same reply, I imagine?"

"But of course. My mercenary friend, this war won't be won today. Maybe tomorrow it'll be *your* turn to lose. You won Europe, you won

Asia. But you haven't won the *world*. You haven't won if it's not over, have you? How do you like those apples, eh?"

Hunter smiled and finished his drink. He didn't lie. He really didn't know where the plans, or Sauer, had gone. But then the Professor's genius wasn't a matter of where, but *when*.

"Shall we?" said Hunter.

The mercenary nodded.

"I get paid either way."

With a squeeze of his calloused trigger-finger the mercenary blew Field Marshall Hunter away.

CHAPTER THREE

Boston, Massachusetts
2017

Franziska Grim was a player of games.

Her education, however, had been a little broader than Henry Brandon's.

She read the instructions by which she led her life one last time, and then set them aside. She would read her next instruction on the day she needed to. She understood the penalty for looking too far ahead. To know too much would not put her life in any more danger than it had been for the last 19 years of her life. Instead, it would be her soul she might lose.

No one should know too much of the future.

How that knowledge must have hurt her father. Such a heavy burden he had carried.

His script, as always, was small and scrawled, the writing of a man whose mind worked faster than his hand.

Redundancy, daughter, in all things.

In this, too. The Nazi may never know who you are, may never foresee their downfall...but we cannot assume a single thing. They must believe this man, John Severance, is dead.

Franziska looked at the ID she'd falsified. Everything would pass a cursory glance. Only the Driver's Licence would not, but they would not check. The Nazi knew the man John Severance was French Canadian, mother still in France, a long-serving member of the European resistance. He would be out in the open just once.

Franziska laid the foundations for a man's death.

The man she chose was an American Nazi collaborator. In the US, he was just a low level functionary serving in local Government, but for the Nazi he was an agent of long standing with a dark track record. She could live with his death.

I never actually killed anyone, she thought.

That would soon change. Her instructions were nearing an end, and with that end, her training would come into play.

A player of games, yes. But everything was a game, wasn't it? Espionage, hacking, picking a lock, stripping down and cleaning a weapon, learning Krav Maga and Jujitsu for nearly twenty years...a deadly game, but still only two choices; win or lose.

CHAPTER FOUR

Middlesex County, Mass.
2017

Henry got in his truck, the seat springs and the suspension both complaining. He drove to town, thought about his decision at the Doctor's practice, and parked 40 yards down the street from the thrift store on the corner.

'Eat more, move less' might well have been his motto until now, but he decided it was high time to turn that around.

It was going to take a while, though –he had to pause in the store to catch his breath.

He found a big rubber band he figured was for exercise or some kind of kinky he didn't have the energy for. The rod holding his spine together felt like a barbell on days like today, and kinky was the last thing on his mind. He remembered what the doctor said. If he eased up on his weight, lost a little of the pot belly, maybe it'd make his back easier.

Maybe.

Less pain he'd buy for a dollar without a quibble. The big rubber band only set him back .75c.

The computer store half a block down had a sign out front:

Digital and Audio on Offer.
Consoles, TVs, VR Headsets.
All at Special Low Monthly Rental Rates!

Even so, something like a VR set'd be more than he got a month in disability, wouldn't it?

He took a seat on a bench looking out across the street, with his stick resting against each knee. He thought about numbers. On his disability check, he was well used to living on a budget, and on his budget there weren't that many numbers to think about.

A minute later he went into the computer store with his giant elastic band over his shoulder. He thought he could run to it. He took out some cash from his worn wallet and asked for the VR set in the window display.

"Rental? Only card for rental."

"Nope," he said. "Not rental. I'll buy it."

"Only that one left," said the store guy. "We've more models out back, but they're only rental."

"I don't want rental," said Henry, who didn't like anything going out monthly, especially as it'd cost him more in the long run. "How much for the display one, then? You'll knock some off for cash, right?"

The guy shook his head. "I have to..."

"No you won't. You'll get the store manager, then do it anyway, because this is an old model, and there are newer, and better. Right? End of line. You don't sell this, it'll be in the dumpster out back, and next month it'll be a Steam Headset, or PS4, or Occulus...something people will actually pay for. What is this? This isn't even Japanese. What is it? Korean?"

"I..."

"$99 dollars? *Really?* I'll give you $40 for the store manager, and a $10 you don't have to tell him about."

Henry took four tens and two fives. The tens he laid on the counter.

The kid (younger than Henry by a couple of decades, probably) had thinning hair and a sallow complexion like he didn't get much sun. He bit his lip, glanced around, then nodded.

Kid, thought Henry. *He's pushing thirty.*

Older you get though, everyone's a kid.

"You know how to use it?"

The kid – *man* – behind the counter eyed the two fives in Henry's heavy fist. "It's for games. Not...you know...*Internet.*"

It took Henry a second to figure out what he was trying to say.

"Sunshine," said Henry. "I know what it's *for*. You think anyone a little crusty round the edges doesn't play? I was a gamer before you were born. I played *DOOM*, I played *Arena* and *Daggerfall* and *Bard's Tale*. I remember *DOS.*'

"I didn't mean that, Sir," said the lad. "Meant...you know...*Pornhub.*"

"That's better is it?" said Henry, and gave the kid a glare. "Today's not going your way, is it?"

"No, Sir. It's really not," said the kid, glancing around for support that wasn't there.

"Think before you speak, eh? After's too late." Henry picked up the set from the glass counter. "And that's the only tip you're going to get today."

Henry pocketed the two fives and took the headset, stalking as fast as a man with two sticks and a rod in his back could go, which, fuelled by anger, was fast enough.

He put the headset and his big rubber band on the passenger seat and muttered around the same volume as the engine of his broke-up, beat-down pick-up truck all the way home.

CHAPTER FIVE

When Henry woke, he turned on his PC.

Before he was married, that was how it had been.

For seventeen years of marriage, his life had been different. Then, he broke his back and a little later, it became the norm for him once more – he would wake and switch on the PC before he set the coffee, before he brushed his teeth or even used the toilet.

The PC wasn't a brand, or a make. It was a mongrel. Didn't even count as a rig, homemade or not. The GPU was an old Radeon and the processor was nearly geriatric (AMD, too, so he could save money).

A desk fan blew air at it so he could run it a little cooler, and it chugged – it wasn't like he needed cooling to overclock. He needed it a little cooler so it didn't catch fire. In the summer, on the hottest day, he'd turn down the settings on whatever he played and put a bowl full of ice cubes between the fan and the back of his case. It wasn't pretty, but it worked.

Weather wasn't a problem right then. Massachusetts, in the autumn? If you were going to skimp on cooling, maybe the Arctic would be better, but it'd do.

Don't need advice from some god damn kid, he thought, still touchy about his encounter at the computer store.

Later, he threw the headset aside in disgust, defeated, and tried to do something, anything, with his exercise band and failed two-for-two.

CHAPTER SIX

Boston, MA.
2017

Grim wasn't Franziska's true family name. Her father changed the family name to Grim when he fled Europe and the Nazi war machine in '70. He'd taken the translation quite literally, and had been one of the few German scientists whose grasp of the English language had been, frankly, terrible.

Her father had been better known as Herr Professor Sauer.

Born in the States in 1980, Franziska had only ten years with her father. He died in '90, the same year the war reached stalemate across the Atlantic and Pacific - the new battlefronts not drawn on land, but on the shifting surface of the two great oceans.

She could have changed her name back, or changed it to anything she wanted it to be, but she liked Grim. It sounded ominous. It was a good name, and it suited her just fine. When she played online (CoD, or sometimes Left 4 Dead 2 if she'd had a bad day) she was GrimReaper, always, even though she often had to add a fair few numbers in there at the end – death was ever popular.

The Professor left her an American name, and she made it her own.

Her name was the first of four things he left to her. The second was her genes.

Franziska's hair was the same colour as her father's – a dull, lacklustre brown. It fell halfway down her back. If people noticed her at all it was her hair people saw, because she tended to slump.

To her, hair was just something which grew on your head.

Her eyesight was 20/20, and her eyes a bold, stark blue. If she did look up from beneath her hair, it was her eyes which stole the show.

Franziska was thin, and though her arms looked like they'd break in a storm (they really wouldn't...she'd been a martial artist since her eighteenth birthday), her gamer callus at the base of her right wrist was probably tough enough to break through walls.

The third thing she received from her father was a house, along with instructions that she was to make it her home from her eighteenth birthday onward, along with enough money so she never had to work.

It wasn't that she'd ever been idle, though, because of the fourth thing, the final thing. The other things *mattered*, of course, but it was the fourth bequest upon which the fate of mankind rested.

It was a long, long letter – one hundred and thirty-two pages, in fact. In those pages, in his tight scrawl, her father detailed every important event of the 20th and 21st century, along with instructions for her, so she might be prepared for what was to come. The letter predicted Franziska's entire future. As for what was to come? The final battle in a war lasting more than 70 years, and the only one which mattered - the last gambit of a dead Professor to bring about the downfall of the Nazi Empire itself.

CHAPTER SEVEN

When she'd used the keys to enter her New England house she found his letter waiting for her, in a manila envelope taped to the clunky keyboard of a Commodore Amiga 3000.

Dearest Daughter, began her father, and told her things she would never have believed in that first page alone. Not mystical things, like her star sign, or her feelings, but solid, inescapable truths. That she wore a red cardigan, from a shop which hadn't existed at the same time as her father, how much it had cost, the day she bought it, and her size.

Solid things. Not guesses, educated or otherwise.

These things, and more than anyone imagines, he told her, *are all possible.*

She kept the first page in a plastic protector, a constant reminder, should she ever need it. She had not.

The last thing on that page was the address – no telephone number – of a tutor who would prove her doorway to the endless worlds and possibilities available because of the CPU and the wonders of silicon.

Call him, her father told her from beyond Death's borders in handwritten, tightly scrawled German. She did, and attended the tutor's private computer class five days a week, three hours a day.

On the second page, which she read later that day, was an admonishment: *Never read the next page until the appointed time. No one should know too much of their future. Remember, Franziska. Look not through the keyhole, lest ye be vexed.*

Later dates in that letter included more; emails, contacts, names, addresses, cell phone numbers, important dates in a long progression of important dates, developments in technology to come...but more importantly, and her father stressed this above all else in her years of preparation: *learn games.*

No explanation, though she was intelligent and understood the focus of his divining centered on microchip technology and computing. A strange field for a scientist to specialise in, she thought, and a Nazi scientist at that. Not bombs, planes, munitions...*games.*

But he had never, ever been wrong.

He'd foreseen Jobs and the GUI, Windows, Kilby's Nobel Prize, MOSFET. He'd seen the rise and rise of Nazism, but never once given Franziska cause to doubt that it *could* end.

The oppression, limitless hatred, the mountains of the dead and the cities left to wild dogs and bones. A world beneath the *Kaiserreich's* black wings *could* be saved. Nazism *could* be defeated. Never be erased, never be forgotten...but one day...

That day would be the day John Severance joined the battle. The man she was destined to meet. The man she was destined to give her life for.

The final entry was dated October 25th...the present day. That day had come. The beginning of the end of Nazism, of the *Kaiserreich*, of her end.

She didn't cry, reading the last words from her father, twenty-seven years after his death.

Take delivery. Read the instructions. Do not deviate. Then, my darling daughter, smile, knowing the light will triumph over darkness, and you will see skies clear of the shadow of the eagle once more.

The doorbell rang.

She pushed herself away from her laptop, and from a keyboard which had come full circle once more - cherry red switches - clunky, like those old Commodore keyboards. Keys you *knew* you'd hit.

The UPS man stood at the door.

The world itself entrusted to the UPS.

She smiled at the thought, but didn't laugh. The UPS man didn't smile back.

"Ma'am. Here," he said, brusque, probably harassed, like most people, and not really looking at her signature on the screen.

They thanked each other, and she closed the door.

A minute later, frowning, she stared at the device in the box. A VR headset, quite unlike anything she'd ever seen before. Underneath that? A game.

PC gamers didn't buy physical games anymore. She didn't know anyone who bought physical. Everyone bought online. *Everything* was digital.

For a man who'd seen the future, it was pretty old school.

But not once had her father made a mistake, and she knew she held in her hands the key to everything. Every part of his work, every part of her life, and the rise of the Reich...

The fall of the Reich.

The resurgence of freedom, of life, of love, of passion, the human soul...

Hope itself rested in a plastic case on a CD-ROM.
The game was called *'ALT-Reich'*.
Franziska turned over the case, and read.

The Nazis are triumphant. You, John Severance, are the last to stand in their way. With an arsenal at your disposal, blast through to victory, or stab your enemies from the shadows.

An open world like no other.
Win your way.
Win any way you can.

This is the final hour, and the world needs YOU...

The cover boasted a garish tableau, bright colours, a muscled man atop a pile of Nazi bodies, a huge gun in one hand and a cigar clenched between teeth like tombstones.

The back cover though didn't feature Uncle Sam below *'...the world needs YOU...'* like of old.

The picture beneath the words was of the earth, shrouded beneath the wings of a giant eagle, the wingspan so large and dark that nearly every corner of the globe fell beneath the shadow, and upon that eagle's back was painted the symbol of dread – the lurid red swastika of the *Kaiserreich.*

CHAPTER EIGHT

Plymouth County, MA.
2017

John Severance walked like a man who knew how to handle himself. Upright, but not with a stick right from ass to neck. Not military but squared away. Fighting in his background, without a doubt, because people who walk like that know they're not going to be rolled on any New England street for their wallet. The kind of man who memorised things in an instant, who was fearless, and smart, but above all a man who looked *dangerous*.

The woman he was supposed to meet stepped from the Greek deli across the street, like she was supposed to. He tapped a newspaper against his leg and walked toward her with a smile because he recognised her for what she was.

*Aryan...*just like him.

Yet instead of giving him a package, as should've been in the script, she shot him square in the face.

Isabella Esposito reached down, pulled aside Severance's jacket and took out his wallet and small pistol while three store owners called 911 and people ran. One kid took photos for Twitter. Another glanced up from a dripping meatball sub, then carried right on eating while tomato sauce ran down his t-shirt.

The wallet was proof enough. The man *was* John Severance...but he didn't have the game.

He was supposed to have a small case, like '90s CD-ROMs. Like Starcraft, like Diablo...but he held nothing.

"Fuck," said Esposito, and her phone rang.

"You screwed it."

"I...he should have it. I did what I was ordered to do."

"No, you were supposed to get the game. You failed the Reich."

"I can make this right," she said.

"Yes," said the voice on the cell phone. *"You can."*

The man holding the cell phone hung up and dropped his phone to the roof of the deli across from Esposito. She was already in his sights. She had been since she stepped into the quiet small town street.

"For the Reich," whispered the man on the rooftop, "but mostly for the money."

His accent was some kind of white African...old Rhodesian blood in there, somewhere. Maybe a South African. It didn't matter. What mattered was the SATO TRG-41, a Finnish rifle, nestling against his left cheek, set for a left-hander. He breathed his will out, and into his finger, and sent the .300 Winchester Magnum round spinning 76 yards at a slight downward elevation through Isabella's head and on, into breezeblock where it stopped.

Overkill, perhaps, but the mercenary wasn't the one who'd fucked up. He hadn't so far.

"Goodbye, Esposito," he said.

He didn't whisper this time, because the street below was filled with everyday Americans roaring and scuttling to and fro in a panic.

A pistol shot didn't worry Americans. Put a sniper on a roof, though, and everyone starts wondering...*who's next?*

CHAPTER NINE

The woman, Esposito, was a Nazi collaborator. The man Esposito thought was John Severance was named David Howe, and unknown to her, he too was a Nazi, formerly of Austria, parents pure Aryan, and his grandparents members of the Nazi party back in the '30.

The trouble with agents, and double agents, and handlers, and compartmentalisation, is that no one really knew who anyone was anymore. Once, wars were fought on battlefields, in uniforms, the lines all neatly drawn. This was scribbles, and all the crayons were the same colour.

Earlier that day, as people still nursed morning coffees, Franziska Grim slipped Howe's wallet from his jacket and took his ID.

Five minutes later, clothes changed, wearing dark glasses and a wig, she emerged from a store doorway and stumbled into Howe, slipping the wallet back.

Three hours a day she'd learned about computers, and code, and programs, and engines. The rest of her time Franziska Grim learned the things a spy would need to know. How to pick a pocket, and how to plant misinformation. *Distraction. Subterfuge.* Tradecraft, Franziska supposed it would be called, though she didn't work for some shady black ops Government branch. Her controller wasn't even alive.

Franziska Grim was alone, and she *was* the front line.

A ten-stone, five-eight woman against an empire spanning the globe.

At 12.30 pm, Franziska pulled off a slightly easier feat. She slid the game, '*ALT-Reich*', into a paper bag carried by a tired-looking, pot-bellied man.

The strange headset – that was for her.

The game was for *him*.

It seemed almost unfeasible to Franziska in that brief moment that after all this time it was this man – one who needed two sticks, and who drove a rusted, dying truck –to whom her father had entrusted the fate of humanity.

Adolf Hitler's '39 to this, the *Kaiserreich's* 2017, and yet, since she first opened that letter taped to a keyboard, her father had *never* made a mistake. Not one, not once. Not even the smallest, tiniest, miscalculation.

Whatever this was, this gambit, it wasn't a thing for spies and soldiers. It was a stratagem for this new battlefield – it was untidy, and chaotic, yes – but now wasn't the time, perhaps, for muscles and big guns...perhaps it was time to give those warriors who wielded gamepads, and controllers, and mice, and keyboards, and VR headsets...their turn at glory.

Is that it, father?

She wondered, like she had so many times, but of course he was never there to answer.

CHAPTER TEN

Middlesex County, MA.
2017

Henry came back from the grocery store with a sad, single man's haul. He was trying to eat better by shopping better...no cookies, chocolate milk...just fruit and simple meals for one.

He felt old.

Three days since Henry bought his VR headset, and still he couldn't figure out how to get it set up. He didn't have a VR game, and he wasn't sure his PC could handle it if he had. A cobbled together PC of a man who lived in small town New England, cooled by ice and a desk fan, running a GPU nearly as old as the dinosaurs in Turok.

Henry Brandon didn't have any kind of faith in his PC. He wasn't a man who believed in faith, but painkillers and hot baths and old games his PC could run without falling over. The newest game he owned was Mass Effect 2, and that was hard enough on his PC. The last game he remembered playing anything on full settings, it was Soldier of Fortune.

Henry didn't have faith in his PC, or himself, or anything else at all. A man on disability, with medical insurance paying out until he was sixty...

Eleven years away.

Eleven years 'til sixty. Once, it had seemed like Mars, or Jupiter, getting old – far distant, irrelevant, alien. Now it seemed like an awful short time.

Henry reached into his grocery bag for a piece of fruit. Instead of an apple, he found something flat, rectangular, and entirely not an apple. He frowned, pulling out a CD-ROM case, packaged like a CD, rather than the larger console, or DVD, or Blu Ray packaging. Like a '90s game, or early '00s.

Still frowning, he read the title aloud.

"*ALT-Reich?* What...?"

Henry turned the case, read the description on the back, frowning, before noting the minimum requirements. His PC was way below, but he didn't give up, because above that was something he'd never seen before:

VR READY.

Henry looked around, like it was some kind of joke. He bought a VR headset, then a VR game about fighting Nazis dropped from...*the sky?*

"Into my bag of apples?"

A man can only frown so long.

Apple and rumbling stomach forgotten, Henry slotted the disk into a CD-ROM drive that whirred and smelled like dust but worked just fine. The screen told him no headset attached. He tried to hit enter, but the keyboard didn't respond, so he put the braided USB cable from his headset into the slot one way, turn, then the same way he'd tried in the first place, and the screen dialogue changed.

Installing new software for your device.

It asked him if he wanted to add a shortcut to the desktop. He didn't, which was good, because the keyboard and mouse both seemed to have fallen asleep.

He heard a voice.

His headphones were hanging from the edge of his old, scarred desk same as usual and disconnected.

It was the headset, without ear cups or buds, which seemed to be talking.

Henry slid the set over his head.

"Oh. My. *Fuck*," he said.

Not long after that, everything but the game just went away...

PART TWO
THE NIGHT OF THE LONG KNIVES

Your new mission: Find the Nazi plans and escape Castle Wolfenstein *alive.*

-

Castle Wolfenstein
– Muse Software/1981

CHAPTER ELEVEN

Green Room
Game Time

"Welcome," said a voice from speakers set in the corners of an austere room. *"John Severance."*

He never read instructions, but Henry remembered well enough who he was supposed to be.

How do I respond? Without his keyboard and mouse, or even a pad, Henry felt lost. He tried nodding, but speakers didn't seem to be designed to *see*, and he couldn't find a fisheye camera up there, hidden away in the plain ceiling.

He wasn't sure if the level design was dumb, or he was.

He tried to move his eyes, wondering if the headset tracked his retina or something else ridiculously clever. That didn't work.

"Yes?" he tried.

That seemed to do the trick.

"Do you wish to undertake the tutorial levels?"

"No," said Henry, feeling like the learning curve of this particular game might be a good few hours at least, but so blown away by the graphics even though he was in a simple room with nothing to move around, or do...it felt *exactly* real.

He thought the effort might just be worth it. Still...who played tutorials? Did new games even *have* tutorials?

Like a '90s game...but with VR?

"Very well. Beginning Level One: The Night of the Long Knives. Immersion level?"

Henry shrugged, imagining immersion was a poetic way of setting a difficulty. He'd been playing games for too damn long to fuss over difficulty. His fingers, if not the rest of him, were heroic.

"Full?" he said, and it must've been the right answer, because the room disappeared faster than he could blink.

CHAPTER TWELVE

Military Base: Location Unknown
Game Time: Prologue

No load screen. Nothing jarring at all. One moment Henry was in the bland room, with a lady's voice calmly speaking to him. The next, here: a chair. He knew he sat, because eye level was lower. He didn't try looking up or down or at himself. He judged an FPS on how detailed his character's hands appeared, and on distant scenery. He didn't think to look. He imagined in the real world his face wore gormless expression - full of wonder.

People'd pay damn good money just to watch people play these things.

"Welcome, John. Still coffee, cream is it?"

The man across from Henry spoke with a British accent Henry only knew from movies and television, and wore a genial smile and a military uniform.

Henry waited for a multiple choice response to come up. Yes, no, he imagined a program could handle...but actual randomised verbal responses?

What the hell?

Keep it simple, he figured. Old school gamer, back in DOS days when you breathed at a game funny and it bugged out, you learned to be a little superstitious about games, and tech, and Henry was of the bash-it-on-the-side-if-doesn't-work generation.

"Coffee? Cream?" asked Henry, sounding and feeling an imbecile. He knew enough to see the chevrons and the medals for marks of rank, but not enough to know what they meant.

"Yes," said the man, patiently. "Dash of scotch once in a while? Did you get hit on the head?"

Did I? I don't know, thought Henry. *Was I supposed to be hit on the head? Do I have amnesia? Seems de rigueur in these sort of situations...*

"No?" he said, desperately trying to find the simplest expressions and shortest words he could, wondering if he should take off the headset and actually bother reading the instructions this time, or bite the bullet and go do the boring-ass tutorial levels.

"Good. Hmm. Good. To business? Sally, bring Mr. Severance a cup of coffee, with cream. Scotch? Seems like that kind of day."

Henry nodded.

Sally leaned forward further than necessary as she poured Henry's coffee. Bright, bold blue eyes assessed him while she poured. Smiling eyes, and he felt himself return the smile.

Sally was very attractive. Thinner than seemed healthy to him, but he guessed women in these things probably catered to an audience a fair bit younger than himself.

Someone took extra care when they designed her.

The thought was laced with an older man's wry humour, rather than a younger man's slack-jawed glee. Maybe he'd felt something watching Lara Croft swim, stuck against a wall in her ridiculous shorts and vest, but he wasn't a kid anymore.

The coffee steamed, too hot, but it was VR so didn't really matter.

It felt so natural to him to return her pleasant smile that he didn't question the *feeling* of smiling in a game where the viewpoint was first person. Only thing of himself he'd ever see were his hands, or maybe his feet...why script something that didn't exist in a game?

These thoughts barely flitted through Henry's mind, though, because the immersion was so complete, so overwhelming, with each second that passed in-game reality was subsumed by the fascination and wonder at something he'd never imagined he would experience in his lifetime. This was Star Trek's holodeck, Philip K. Dick. Something with Tom Cruise starring, looking serious and smarmy all at once.

John - *no, I'm Henry* - raised his hand to sip his coffee.

In his threadbare living room, Henry didn't move, because this wasn't, exactly, virtual reality.

In the game, he swore he could taste the coffee, feel the heat, the delicate China (so very British...) in his hand.

"I won't lie, John," said the man before him. "This is one hell of a mission. The final throw of the dice. All those who oppose the *Kaiserreich* - every operative, every cell, every man and woman on God's green earth who dream of a free dawn...*everything* depends on your success."

"That's a shit-ton of pressure," said Henry, forgetting to worry about glitches, or bugs. Speech responses already felt as natural as multiple dialogue paths on a screen.

"Of course," said the soldier. "Not dying. That's paramount. Can't save the world if you're dead, can you?"

"No. I suppose not," said Henry.

No reloads? Save points? Some kind of quicksave feature?

The thought slid right on by, like his hunger and his aching back on a couch back in the real world, and was gone.

The next thought was somewhere below, outshone by the wonder of the game itself.

If it's a game, and I die, it's just reality, isn't it?

"The aeroplane's fuelled and ready and waiting on you. Kit's on the plane. Godspeed, and good luck."

To go where? he thought.

"Wait...what? I..."

It must have been a cut scene, though. Sight, sensation, and sound switched seamlessly from the warm office and good coffee to the bouncing seat of a military transport plane.

CHAPTER THIRTEEN

Over the North Sea, Europe.
Game Time: 00:00
Achievements Enabled.
Immersion Full
Difficulty: COME GET SOME.

A man swayed, standing before Henry, grinning.
"First time on a plane?"
"No, "said Henry. He hadn't actually been on a plane or outside the U.S.A."First time without a cute stewardess, though," he added, because he thought it sounded like the kind of thing a man named John Severance, saviour of the world, might say.
Might as well roll with it.
The man laughed. "And I made an effort, too."
This is amazing.
The man's accent was strange, but American, somewhere.
"American?" asked Henry.
"By way of lots of different places, you know? Been a soldier for a long time. Salvador, Peru, Alaska, Wales, Italy, Morocco. Spent the best part of my life fighting the bastards, it seems."
"Nazis?"
The man gave Henry a quizzical look, the kind of perfect game designers could only dream of.
"Ah...pulling my leg. Picked that little expression up from a Scottish filly in...Christ. '09?"
Wistful. The man gazed, as though at the past and a Scottish filly, maybe dead now, in a huge war against the Nazis that wasn't real, because the Reich were stalled, right?
The world might be gone, but the U.S.A. and the U.S.S.R stepped out of that fight, didn't they? Australia, which belonged to the Nazis, and America's own New Zealand stared across the sea at each other for

nearly a decade. Japan, annexed by the U.S.S.R, gazed down on both from a lofty height, like eyes looking down at a nose and mouth. A distant, detached stalemate that worked well enough to stop the entire world imploding.

The U.S.A. didn't fight this fight, not anymore, because the Nazis *won*, didn't they?

They won most of the world, and the power, and the U.S.A. held what it had while trade, politics, economies all ferried back and forth between towering blockades of Navy steel from coast to coast and through satellites and fibre optics.

"The Captain..."

"Captain?"

"General?" tried Henry.

"Captain General? What is this, the '90s? Doesn't exist. The Royal Family of England hasn't existed since...'89? And that was Marine. You mean the Brigadier. I forget...you're not army, right?"

"Right?" said John.

"Hell of a record, though."

Is it? Henry had no idea.

"The Brigadier said you'd have some kit for me?" said Henry, trying to stick to a script that had been written entirely without subtitles. "Weapons and such?"

"Yes, right."

The well-travelled man held out a knife in a leather sheath.

"A...knife? Can't I have a gun?"

"A gun?" The man laughed again and Henry raised his eyebrows as he took the knife. It didn't seem all that funny to him.

CHAPTER FOURTEEN

A different man came from someplace closer to the cockpit. Maybe it was cosy. Henry didn't know, but he imagined a man as dapper as this didn't ride next to the engines.

"Bonsoir, Monsieur. Mr. Severance?" added the man, a Frenchman. Henry understood that much, otherwise, France was just somewhere *over there*.

Henry shook his head.

"My apologies, Mr. Severance. I was informed you spoke several languages. No matter, non? Nazi sympathisers, Nazi spies...*Nazis*. Nazis here, Nazis there?" The Frenchman shrugged expressively. "Tonight, we take the first step toward making the eagle flightless. Tonight, we cut the wing from Europe."

Henry tried to concentrate on what he figured amounted to the rundown of his mission as he bounced around on magnificent physics - low down through turbulence, flying at speeds he didn't even know were possible, toward Holland. It was hard to think, and listen, and look. The whole experience was overwhelming.

Then for the first time he saw something hazy around the Frenchman's head, like an aura, and realised he hadn't *fought* anyone at all. The glitch, the slowing in his ancient GPU, whatever it was, it slammed him back from the game so hard he remembered not only that this was a game...but that his body was in his living room, drooling on his couch.

How long's it been? Ten minutes? And I haven't punched, stabbed, or shot a single person?

Strange for an FPS. Getting used to movement, maybe, but that didn't take long. WASD, a mouse, that was about the basics.

Maybe something else is going behind the scenes?

Like a co-op. Like the other player hit the action, and he hit the exposition?

He had no way of knowing. The entire experience was alien, new as a television to some tribesman recently discovered some place like Borneo, who was probably perfectly happy without one.

Was this just the developers showing off?

"Monsieur..." said the Frenchman and that was all he said, because something hit the plane and tore the front and back apart and the Frenchman was vaporised in a spray of blood and bone that seemed to hang in the air, then, with the sudden roar of wind and engine and fire, was gone.

Henry grinned.

Here we go, he thought, readying to jump from the burning plane into a hail of bullets and...

The screen turned black.

"Fuck!"

He yanked the headset free and smelled himself, his stale sweat and breath within the headset, but mostly the nasty stench of hot plastic. His PC was smoking.

"Shitfire crapshit shit shit!" he yelled, like a good swear would stop the whole thing catching fire.

CHAPTER FIFTEEN

Middlesex County, MA, USA
2017

It wasn't the blue screen of death, but black, like death and oblivion. His living room stank. He didn't try to turn the PC back on. It was hot enough to leave it alone and say a prayer.

He'd imagined around ten minutes of game time had passed, but it was full dark, he needed the toilet, and he was ravenous. The first time he looked at a clock, it was the flashing LED on his microwave.

Five hours?

Later, he sat at his metal-legged kitchen table eating a meal from the very same microwave, thinking not about his numb legs, or going to sleep, or how long he'd just spent in a shooter and not actually *shot* anyone.

He wondered if the game had saved, or if he had to fight the beachhead against the Nazis to reach a save point, and finally get a gun. Younger, he'd probably have been raging about a cooked GPU and maybe losing his progress, but strangely, the thought of going through the entire introduction all over again didn't faze him at all. He wondered just how adaptable the engine was.

Could he throw his coffee in the Brigadier's face, or refuse his mission, or stab the Frenchman and force the plane to dive bomb, Kamikaze, into the sea?

Suicide, like jumping off a cliff just to find the edge of a world and see the sights on the way down, or to escape the town guard because you killed a stupid chicken?

Curiosity was fine when you had quick save.

Good spot to finish, he thought. Saved or not, he figured he could always skip through the beginning and figure it out.

Next up, exploding plane, and *surely* some action?

He stood on legs still numb and stupid, but before his legs remembered what they were about, someone rapped their knuckles on his front door.

Nearly midnight, someone knocking at your door, even in a quiet town in Massachusetts, Henry's first instinct was to pretend he wasn't in. But he'd just been John Severance, international...*whatever*...and as such he still felt bold. Just a gamers' hangover, of course, like when he played in any FPS for too long, and the halls and doorways of his own home shimmered, and hestrafed unthinkingly into the kitchen or the bathroom, until the feeling subsided.

He checked the peephole.

A girl stood back from the door respectfully – slight build, long hair, and not threatening in the slightest.

Maybe it's a set-up, he thought, then laughed. *Getting a bit carried away, Henry.*

It wasn't until he opened the door and the light from his living room lit up her bright blue eyes that the jolt, like electricity, ran through him.

The girl...the woman...from the game.

She beat him to the punch, and this time, her words knocked the wind right out of him.

"John? John Severance?"

"No...what? Wait...*Sally*?"

"What? No..." said Franziska. "No...oh. Shit."

CHAPTER SIXTEEN

Across the street, shrouded in shadows, a man watched Franziska enter Henry's house. The mercenary had been in the employ of the *'Reich'* since his teens, and now, nearing seventy, he was still one of their best operatives...if not the best. A seventy-year old man's body, yes, but augmented, replaced...*improved.*

He smiled, watching the door close, hefted a bag on his shoulder and stepped into the light when he saw a curtain twitch from the corner of his eye.

Nice neighbourhood. Low crime. Ergo, nosy neighbours.

He checked his watch.

Still time...still time.

The mercenary walked to the house with the twitchy curtains and knocked. His knuckles were scarred, some replaced by high-density ceramics and metal alloys, and much, much sturdier than the girl Franziska's. *His* knock was hard enough to rattle the door in the frame.

The spy hole darkened and he smiled warmly.

"County Detective, ma'am. Sheriff's department. Sorry for the late hour."

He assumed it was a woman, because he thought women were nosier than men. His experience, while not based on science, exactly, was rooted in decades of killing for money all over the world.

"Detective?" said a lady who was older than the mercenary, and a sight less spritely.

"I apologize for the late hour, ma'am, but we're checking the neighbourhood. Armed robbery earlier this evening. Just making sure the residents are safely tucked in."

"Well, that's very kind."

"Our job, ma'am. Do you have someone else there, or do you need a car on the street? Pardon me, but we have to look after our ladies," he tipped an imaginary hat and she smiled.

"No...my husband passed, God rest him. Just me and my sweet poochie.'"

"Terrible shame, ma'am," he said, thinking no such thing as he took her head in both hands and wrenched swiftly, breaking her neck.

He dropped her back in the porch and shoved her clear of the door with his boot.

"Ma'am," he said, closed the door and checked his watch.

Still time.

Already, the Night of the Long Knives would have begun, any resistance hamstrung before the first missile even flew.

He moved to Henry Brandon's house, stride sure and steady on legs firmly muscled and mostly metal bones.

CHAPTER SEVENTEEN

For the first time in her life, Franziska was lost, rudderless. Her father got this *wrong*.

Of all the things to get wrong? Of all the places for it to fall apart? The final battle in a war spanning nearly seven decades...and he screwed this? This?!

"You're supposed to be John Severance. I mean...*really* John Severance."

"What? I'm..."

"Who are you?'"

"What? You knocked on my door, lady."

"Don't *lady* me," said Franziska, and scooted past Henry into the house. "Close the door. I don't know who might be watching...I don't know *anything*. He never got it wrong before. *Never*."

She dumped herself into his place on the couch, and he was forced to stand up in his own house.

"Is this about the game? I found it, all right? If it's supposed to be someone else's I can just give it back."

"You can't, because there is no one else. Now it's you. You played it, didn't you? You knew me."

"In the game you're Sally. What is it, some kind of co-op thing? I'm online, and I didn't know. Are they allowed to do that?"

"Shut up. *Listen*."

"You shut up. You're in *my* house. In the middle of the night. In *my* seat. Mine."

"What are you, twelve?"

"What are you, eleven?"

"Fuck's sake," said Franziska, and put her head in her hands.

"Try again," said Henry. "One minute, and I'm going to throw you out. I'm out of shape, but I've got five stone on you. At least."

"Yeah, you have. First ten seconds – the war against the Nazis? Against the Reich?"

"In the game."

"No, dipshit. The war. *The* war. *This* war.'"

"It's over. Stalemate. Nagasaki accords. Blockades, no-fly zones, dead man's land, lines drawn somewhere out there in the ocean and north and south, too, in frozen places. Dipshit? Get out."

"Touch me and I'll snap both your arms and stuff you in the fridge."

"What?"

Henry took a step back, because she suddenly looked at him and those blue eyes didn't waver at all. He believed she could actually do it.

She could, too.

"It's *not* over," she said, as forcefully as she'd threatened him. "It's never been over. In The Nazi war machine is advancing again, and this time American soil is their goal."

"Bullshit."

"My dad...he...told me."

"What, he's high up in the *Kaiserreich*, is he? Whatever. It's done. We're sitting here, they won the world and no one stands because what is there left? *They own the entire world.* And still, get out of my house, damn it."

"Not exactly," she said, ignoring him completely. Her father was dead, and now he'd got something as important as this guy wrong?

"Mr...who are you?"

"My name is Henry Brandon, and this is my house, and..."

"I know the drill. Get out, blah blah. Let's try this again. That thing work?" she said, rising and sniffing the back of his PC. "Smells like it was just burned at the stake for being a witch. Is it a witch?"

"It works...*what*? Jesus."

"My name is Franziska Grim," she said, turning those arresting blue eyes full beam back on him. "My father was a professor who specialised in programming and game theory. He created that game, and people will kill for it. Probably have. The war you think is over, isn't. Televisions, the news, the internet...everything they're fed is controlled by Governments, and Governments are controlled by corporations...and you believe the words forced into the mouths of talking heads on the television?"

"I don't have a television, and you're insane. I'm calling the police."

"Give me a chance. Please. *Please.* I'm lost as you right now but if you believe nothing...people *will* kill for this. Please. I'll beg if you want. I'll pay you if that's what you want. I'll blow you and pretend to like it if that's what it takes, but please plug in."

Henry stared back. The only light in the room was a standing lamp in the corner, and those eyes seemed brighter than the lamp, and there were tears in her eyes, too.

She's desperate.
For what...he didn't know.
For a game? For a war that's been done for over a decade?
Or, she was just plain crazy.

"Lady...Ms. Grim? I can see you need this...I believe you might be in some kind of shit, either that, or schizophrenic. Even though you're in my house, in the middle of the night, and insane, and maybe you can break my arms...I'm still not putting that thing back on."

"Because it's *too* real, right? The game? It's too real, isn't it? Believe what you want, but you're all I've got and you have absolutely zero poker face, by the way."

"I'm your only hope?" he said, laughing though it wasn't funny.

"If you like," she said. "There isn't much time, and less while you flap your chatter."

She pulled a lurid pink laptop from the bag she carried. "Your rig won't handle two sets, and I'm coming in, too. Let me show you, and maybe...maybe you'll believe. If not? If there's nothing? I promise you I'll leave. You'll never hear from me again."

"What do I care?"

"You'll never hear from me, Mr. Brandon, because if you don't put the fucking set only America won't exist anymore."

"You think your dainty pink laptop...?"

"Because it's pink? Because I'm a *woman?* If this thing were a plane, it'd hit Mach IV. It'd be a record breaker. You want to save the world or be a dick?"

"No," said Henry bluntly. "Not really. I want you out of my house, and ten hours sleep. I'm not a man in the game. I'm Henry Brandon and you're a nut."

"Possibly," she said. "Look at the case," she said, and stood, and snatched the headset from his desk and jammed the USB into her laptop first time. "See a developer's name? A logo? *Anything?*"

"...no. So what, it's a bootleg..."

"It's not the prohibition. Christ, you're slow. It's not a game about big fucking guns. It *is* the gun. The game is a weapon."

"What?"

Henry shook his head, and moved to the door.

"You're gone."

"Screw this," she said, and kicked him hard in the back of his knee, ducked under his arm, spun him and dumped him onto his couch. She punched him in the solar plexus, a hard blow with her left, and a knife hand strike to his sternum and the same time with her right hand.

Henry's breath was gone, and if he had any fight, ever, he certainly didn't right then.

She jammed the VR set on his head.

"Sorry about that. Don't have a heart attack, OK? I'll meet you on the other side."

As an afterthought, she added, "I promise I won't tweet pictures of you drooling," then flicked a switch on his set. "Probably."

That tiny switch sent Henry reeling away from pain and breathlessness and yes, fear. It fired him along some kind of electronic pathways from his couch, all the way back into a world he didn't understand. But right then, his own world had become just as much a mystery as...

CHAPTER EIGHTEEN

North Sea
Game Time Elapsed: 00:37.

...this.

The living room, the rude mad woman, even the constant ache of the rod in Henry's back, disappeared. This wasn't just immersion, but crashing into freezing water, the shock and this new reality so stunning he lost his breath, panicked and sank as he hit the North Sea, the stretch of water separating a fallen England and the rest of a Nazi Europe.

Henry floundered until he broke the surface. The brine, the sting of salt in his eyes, the cold, the taste. Huge waves pummelled him, every sensation overwhelming in intensity. He panted, terrified, convinced he was going to die. Game or couch, everything forgotten but one moment, when the harsh cold of the sea was replaced by fire and wind. The entire sky seemed filled with burning airplanes, explosions, fuselage, wing, gunner's towers, engines, oil on fire on heavy seas, or shining metal falling through the sky toward him.

The wreckage of his plane was spread above and below the sea. No screams, no survivors.

He wanted out.

Henry Brandon had never learned how to swim. He couldn't talk, or make commands, or move, or interact with this world in anyway. Panic at the cold and the crash and the sea stole everything away. The whole of existence – real and virtual, reduced to a tiny, pure point of sheer terror.

He reached out to take off his helmet – not a WWII tin hat you could boil tea in, but a modern polymer thing. He yanked at the combat helmet. It wasn't coming off, and taking both arms from the water to try was a mistake. You can't float in armour, you can't swim without your arms, and you damn sure can't do anything when you're full of panic and breathing in salt water off the coast of...*Holland?*

Anti-aircraft guns fired heavy tracers at the squadron which had flown alongside Henry's own transport. A city levelled during the early days of this terrible war was burning again.

Calm down. Calm...calm...

He told himself this, slapping the water, taking huge gulps of air each time he surfaced.

I can't swim, but...he can.

It's just a scene. The opening. The action. Now. I storm the beach, rifle in hand.

I haven't got a rifle, he thought, and sputtered out salt water once more, panic making him heavy.

The game'll fix that, won't it? Here, the destructible scenery, there, gibs flying all around. Don't forget the sound devs, right? The deafening roar of shells and plumes of sand...boom!

Brilliant!

This is Normandy...Medal of Honour style – only with better graphics. And...

It wasn't Normandy, but Rotterdam.

Henry Brandon might have been scared, but here?

I'm John Severance, international Nazi killing badass.

The warmth below Henry's waist belied that.

But, *whatever*, he thought. He forced himself to straighten up, to man up, to fight, because...

Badasses piss themselves, too.

He could ignore the cold, and the fire, because it was bullets which killed, not the scenery. Henry couldn't swim, or tread water, but *John* could. Of course he could. Severance could probably fly a plane with no hands as long as he had a Playboy centrefold for inspiration.

Henry swam. He imagined a game with no stamina bar, and didn't seem to tire.

Finally, grinning (or just frozen), his feet hit foreign soil. *Nazi* soil. He raised his hand, imagining a decent gun there, a Garand, or a Thompson, or a...

But this wasn't the past. This was the present.

Armalite, he thought. *Anything'll do. Seriously. Heckler and Koch? Smith and Wesson?*

Nothing.

There were no weapon hotkeys here. He couldn't hit 1, or 2, or roll a mouse wheel...and even if he could, he didn't have a gun.

His inventory included a knife, and nothing else.

He high-kneed through the shallows until he reached firm ground, then, hit full stride and ran crazily along the short stretch of coast toward the lights of the port city. He ran anywhere tracer fire wasn't. Planes flew in from the sea, roaring jets, but...

Is that a Stuka?

It was. A *Junkers Ju 87* - a Nazi bomber long out of service.

This one, though, was pimped out and it wasn't dropping bombs, but strafing, banking, and letting loose with a barrage of missiles, like a modern fighter jet but one out of time - a Pinto with a Bentley engine. The sight was jarring enough Henry remembered who he was. He might not ache here, and maybe overweight with a tired heart didn't matter when you were no more than code...but *what the...?*

He stared at the dinosaur in the sky when something screamed from out to sea toward the bunkers and tanks waiting for Severance's special, early, retirement party. A missile, something serious, and fast enough awareness of its passage lasted no more than a second. The aftermath, though...

A ground shaking explosion blew whatever stood at ground zero into the air - walls, reinforced concrete, bricks and rubble, shards of tanks that could take depleted Uranium shells, but not whatever the hell just hit them.

This was something fired from a sub, or an aircraft carrier, or a destroyer, or the fist of God himself.

Henry dragged himself from the dirty sand, at the end of a furrow he'd made when the concussive force blew him back.

Inventory? Knife. Check. Arms and legs? Check.

This time, being armed with only a knife didn't seem quite so bad - who needs an assault rifle when a bona fide Holland-Destroyer's got your six?

From terror, to awe, to joy, Henry's emotions ran parallel to the carnage on a path laid out for him. Not on rails, but not an open world, either. The carnage on his right, the sea on his left. North or south were the only choices, and from his helmet a small, solid voice came through.

'Engage the HUD, Mr. Severance.'

The game will provide.

He fumbled with the combat helmet and a screen descended over his left eye, the display transparent but for a light green readout. A location marker appeared – him – and his objective. Direction only, no map. Him in green, surrounded by red markers on a spinning compass.

Enemies, and lots of them.

He ran, getting used to watching the HUD and checking his surroundings, too, puffing until he remembered he didn't have to. Being in bad shape was a hard habit to forget. He'd gone slow for most of the fourth decade, either through pain or fear of his heart quitting on him.

But this was a game, and a *great* one. There wasn't a stamina bar on the HUD, nor a health bar. The absence of one meant he didn't have to run out of steam. He could sprint every-goddamn-where. The absence of the other? What does *that* mean?

'It means there are no reloads, Mr. Severance,' said the voice in his helmet.

"Who are you?"

'What. I am an Artificial Military Intelligence program. You may call me Amy.'

"Well, Amy...I could run from here to the objective, but I'd rather drive. Can you highlight a car?'"

'No cars in the vicinity. However, should you be able to drive a tank...'

Bullets pinged and ricocheted all around. The red dots were drawing closer, and he was out in the open, lit up by fire.

"I'll figure it out, Amy," he told the voice in his helmet, trying to sound confident. Feeling confident. A game like this? Storming a country through some kind of explosion programmed so perfectly he still felt the shock in his bones.

Hell, I can still feel sand in my underwear.

'Understood. Closest match: Ulan IFV. And...updating objective.'

CHAPTER NINETEEN

Rotterdam, Holland.
Game Time: 00:55.

Henry slammed against the side of the tank. If he had a stealth bar, he figured he just drank it dry – every red dot on his HUD swarmed toward his small, very lonely, green arrow.
"How do I get in, Amy?"
'Armaments restricted to a single dagger? I suggest knocking politely, or cupcakes.'
Brilliant. Smart arse. Why does everything have to be a character?
"It's manned?"
'What use would a tank be with no crew?'
"You didn't say I'd have to fight my way in."
'I see no other option. This vehicle contains the minimum number of crew an Ulan IFV: Driver, Gunner, Commander.'
Here we go, then, he thought and clambered up over the tread arches, to the roof, and knocked on the top hatch - entirely the wrong thing to do, it turned out. A man crawled from someplace beneath the vehicle, saw Henry and fired high and wide. It wasn't a warning shot – he just missed. Soldiers don't have to yell 'stop', or 'halt', or read Miranda rights. The enemy soldier fired again. His next shot bounced from the armoured body, pinging away into the sky and startling Henry so he fell off balance, slid and stumbled and landed feet first on the Nazi's shoulders, driving him to the ground. Something in the Nazi's shoulder cracked, and Henry thought, *clavicle, partial fracture, AC joint tear, right hand useless, roll right, stab down,* like a read out, instant, in his head. A catalogue of injuries and attack choices hardwired into his, or Severance's capabilities. He didn't have time to think or question why or how he would know that, or how detailed a simulation, how deep immersion could be for a developer to consider the tiniest crack of a fragile bone breaking. He didn't have time to analyse. Almost

instantaneously, it seemed, as he landed the knife in his hand already jutted at a horrible angle between the man's neck and trapezius muscle.

Spine severed, bleeding out, heart slowing, stopping, dead.

Killing. Like a waterslide with bumps. Over in a jiffy. Fun for all the kids!

The light from the rear hatch of the Ulan highlighted Henry to each red enemy sprinting toward his position.

'Two more crew inside. I suggest...'

He didn't need Amy's input at that point.

Henry crawled in, stabbed the first man he met in the minimal space for transport at the rear. He had to slice at an awkward angle up and across – there wasn't enough clearance overhead to strike downward. Henry's blade took the man in the wrong lung for instant death, but close enough to do the job.

Air whistled as he yanked his knife free and cut the man's throat from behind.

Hard, quick, and harsh, and Henry barely had a chance to consider what he was doing. His body – Severance's body – was cruising.

The dying man gurgled out his last breath, and there was a question in the man's eyes. He wanted to ask...something.

The guy couldn't speak. Henry found he was glad. He didn't want to imagine what a dying man might have to say to his killer.

Bring the kids, they said. Kill some Nazis, they said...

No wonder people didn't like too much reality in their games.

The man in the driver's seat didn't get a chance to turn, or draw his side arm. Henry's angle was better. The driver was laid back in a bucket seat, and Henry's knife slid easier than he'd imagined through -

external carotid, internal jugular, sternomastoid muscle

until the tip of his bloodied dagger hit the -

articular capsule between C4 and C5 vertebrae of the cervical spine.

There was a pinging noise inside his helmet, then, a small fanfare.

'Insta-kill!' said a small, tinny voice from somewhere inside the helmet. Not Amy. No more than a sound effect, this.

I just levelled up?

It wasn't until he dragged the driver to the side and back from the bucket seat that he wretched from a body which shouldn't be able to vomit *because it didn't eat.*

The driver was a woman, and what had felt far too real already now felt disgusting. Nerves completely severed, nothing to hold her jaw in place, the driver's face was lopsided, and one eye was shut. Like she was winking.

You can't be sick in a game.

"Amy? This *is* a game...right?"

'I don't understand the question, John. Please elaborate, and perhaps while driving. Seven armoured vehicles converging. Firing range in thirty...'

"A little help!"

'Twenty-eight...'

"Amy!"

Some kind of heavy explosive hit and detonated close enough to rock the tank and Henry was back, worrying about dying, not about killing.

'Austrian-Spanish Ulan IFV. Schematics uploading...transferring...'

A huge amount of text began to scroll across the HUD – far too much to read. Blueprints, details, vehicle history, development, mechanical schematics.

"Amy, I don't need Jane's. It's not Rainbow Six."

'John?'

He slid into the seat and wiped the blood from his hands.

"Forget that...how do I make it *go*?"

'Directional controls similar to those of a motorcycle are standard, including throttle. Six-speed gearshift, forward and reverse. Floor brake which I suggest you refrain from using.'

Playing violent games never bothered him before. Why now?

'Incoming, John.'

He twisted the throttle and the Ulan jolted forward hard enough to jar his neck...and it *hurt.*

Because it had been guilt free before. Zombies, aliens, enemy soldiers...humanity stripped away, just fodder for his latest gun.

Shells exploded beside the tank, the sound of shrapnel and rubble against the hull stark and shrieking, while the diesel engines roared and the tank bucked, accelerating all the time.

These are Nazis...they're not human. They're still just bullet-magnets...right?

He could feel the wetness, the warmth, the way the blood was already working into the creases in his hands...he could feel that blood, and pain, sickness, disgust, wonder, elation, fear...

Focus, John. It's a game, and you've a job to do...

Perhaps it was because of those emotions, overwhelming in their intensity, and maybe all the munitions exploding behind, left, right, ahead of him, that Henry missed the first moment he thought of himself as John.

CHAPTER TWENTY

The HUD view changed. Amy laid out a road map for Henry, and now it was about speed, and nerve.

He was driving a God-damn tank. He felt he should be yelling with glee – an overweight middle-aged man in an epoch where technology had surely reached the zenith of possibility. Not driving a tank with a game pad, or a keyboard...but with *his hands*. With every one of his senses, too - the engines straining at nearly 70 km/h was deafening, the stench awful but amazing at the same time, the shuddering of a ton of metal and treads and destructive beauty shaking Henry's every joint, his jaw, and battering clenched teeth.

This was the stuff of miracles, science fiction, make-believe, mankind's true potential...but still he couldn't shake it.

Guilt.

He was forty-nine years old and he hadn't felt guilty about anything except a marriage that had slipped through his fingers. He didn't enjoy the feeling at all.

And the tank itself?

Henry had always hated driving games. He liked RPGs and shooters and when he wanted a slow night or day he tended to play turn-based strategy. It was a cosy thing for a man who grew into games with Might and Magic and Command and Conquer.

For Henry, before even BFGs and the moons of Mars, it had been hexes, and earlier iterations still, back to 8-bit computing. Jumping a frog between cars - that, he could do.

The tank was astounding...but driving it? He was terrified. Still the frog, but now he was trying to avoid walls, houses, embankments, traffic signals, follow a map over his left eye, use controls he wasn't used to, while tank munitions smashed into and through anything and everything.

He followed the HUD, and Amy, and barely looked at his surroundings. Part of the ache in his jaw was down to the vibrations. The rest was all him, clamping his teeth together.

He took turns, following the neon glow of his HUD map, while enemy fire raked the armoured hide of the vehicle.

Finally, he turned, and gained maybe five seconds grace before his pursuit blew him to pieces, him, melted into a bucket seat for future generations to marvel at in some museum, maybe.

'Your objective is through the gate ahead. Straight run.'

Speed and weight against weight and strength. Acceleration, velocity, force, mass...

The Ulan was running seventy km/h.

'Even at max speed, John, this tank might not break...'

"Don't worry about it," he said.

For a moment, Henry relished the idea of literally crashing out of the game. But he didn't. At the last minute he swerved.

An enemy shell blew out the concrete beside the gate and he yanked the handle, throttled back, ignored the gears and braked hard, like a stunt driver sliding into a parallel parking slot, and side-swiped the tank into the crumbling wall.

He ended half-up on concrete, stranded.

A terrible machine of war no more useful than an upside-down tortoise. The rear hatch was jammed shut against the wall. Even so, the Ulan might have been able to get clear...with someone better qualified at the controls.

I bet the woman I killed could've done it, he thought, and wished he could forget that already.

He could sit and wait for a shell to find its mark, or he could move. He moved. He didn't care if he died in the game and crashed out without saving.

He did care if he *really* died...and at this point he wasn't sure shell *here* wouldn't end him *there*.

While his mind might have been confused, as though it existed in two places at once, John Severance's body knew exactly what it was about. It wanted to live, and more.

It wanted to *win*.

Henry Brandon bathed in guilt while John Severance's hand reached down and took the tank driver's side arm for his own. Henry saw her awful expression - her sightless eyes, the terrible gash through her neck, her slack features, and somehow worse; his sick beneath her.

John Severance hefted her sidearm and burst from the top hatch, jumped down to the ground inside the compound the Ulan breached, and ran.

If it was to be a choice between getting shot or shooting Nazis...

Franziska, Henry remembered. Those startling blue eyes. She hadn't exactly said *ALT-Reich* was a game, had she?

John's boot and Henry's mind, or maybe here they were the same thing, lashed out and kicked in a grand old wooden door beneath a porch of stone and Doric columns.

She said it was a weapon.

CHAPTER TWENTY-ONE

Middlesex County, MA
2017

The Afrikaner mercenary's boot smashed Henry Brandon's door open hard enough to dent the plaster on the wall behind the handle. He followed his gun into the room.

Franziska spent twenty years learning how to fight, and how to shoot, and that was plenty long enough to understand she couldn't punch a bullet, or flip on its back.

"Smart girl," said the Merc. At his age, most people were young enough to be boys and girls. "Small town doors, eh? Hardly worth a boot. City door, now...that's a different thing. Franziska Sauer?"

She didn't see any point in denial. She nodded.

"Sit down, Ms. Sauer. I understand you prefer *Grim*. How pleasant it is to meet the esteemed, though sadly deceased, Herr Professor Sauer's lovely daughter. You hide your light under a bushel, eh? You really are quite an attractive lady."

"Fuck you," she replied.

"Unfortunately, you have that backwards. You and Mr...Severance? Yes. Severance. It is you two who are...*fucked*. Such a colourful and backward land, your America."

"Who are you?"

The mercenary dumped his bag from his free shoulder, and moved further into the room so he could cover Franziska and the drooling middle aged man with his pistol.

"I believe I am...the enemy. The *antagonist*. The one who steals the family away in the opening reel of the Saturday morning picture show, or the...game? Games..." the Merc shook his head. "So much of this future I do not quite comprehend, eh? So much I do not like."

He shrugged, and smiled, and raised his hands genially.

"A hero must have a foil, eh? A nemesis. An opposite, if you will. You see, Ms. Grim, while you work in the shadows for the light, I work in the light for the darkness. You understand? Ah, of course you do. We are not fools, eh? Still..."

With his pistol pointing at Franziska, he tapped Henry's headset. "This is reality, and virtuality, and alternity...this is *everything*, is it not? *This* is the battlefield."

Henry, slumped on his couch, was unresponsive.

The mercenary flicked his pistol left, right, like the pistol had personality, and shook its head.

"I would like to have met Dr. Sauer. A remarkable mind."

"Killing me won't stop this. He is already in the game."

"...and the game is all things, yes. I understand. I kill either of you here, and you both simply meld with the game, eh? I chase down nothing more than lines of programming. But with your bodies dead here, and your minds dead in the game, eh? Then it ends."

Franziska's eyes widened, ever so slightly.

"You hide your surprise quite well, but not well enough. Your father made more than one mistake. He hid the plans away, and saw you, his *avatar*. Ha. But in so many years he thought the *Kaiserreich* could not decipher, could not untangle, that kernel of an idea? The Professor was a savant, yes...but the Nazis - their resources extend across the world, eh? Decades to duplicate his work. Their efforts...perfect? Perhaps not. The Nazis lack innovation, certainly...but they have plenty of wildly brilliant minds at their disposal."

"You're too late, whoever you are. The world is now *his*." She spoke of Henry Brandon, not John Severance. If the mercenary did not know this was not John Severance, that John Severance was an invention of her father's world, she would not tell him.

"This man with his pot belly? My career is nearly as long as the *Kaiserreich* itself. Oh, I can kill him. I *will*."

Franziska said nothing.

"Good," said the Merc. "I like a woman who dies well. Now, hold still. This, Ms. Grim, is the most wonderful invention of our age. Not your alternate realities, and virtual realities, but simple duct tape."

He began to bind her, and she could do nothing against his gun and hands far stronger than they should be.

"You can fix all manner of ills with the liberal application of duct tape," he said, and prepared to send them both to *ALT-Reich*. Not virtual, not real, but alternate. A trip *sideways*.

CHAPTER TWENTY-TWO

Rotterdam
Game Time: 01:06

'Course it's just a game. A game gives you a knife, you get a pistol, you get a submachine gun, then an assault rifle. Level ups, without the levels...right?
It's a game, or it's not a game...this, though. This isn't my body.
That much, Henry did know. His body would never be able to do the things he was doing.
Is this even my mind?
Now that, he didn't know. He thought that perhaps the woman called Franziska didn't know, either, and that troubled him just as much as the stark bright reality of this game.

What he did know, without question, was what a game did *not* do. A game did not give you a *tank* instead of a pistol. You kicked in huge double doors of one of Rotterdam's oldest and grandest buildings to survive the early days of the war, the Witte Huis, you were supposed to be met by a sweeping double staircase. The enemy would hold the high ground, and stand around like mannequins while you raked a machine gun back and forth. You did not, *not ever*, find a long, dark, narrow hallway after a doorway like that.

But that's what he had to work with. What else was there to do? Each time he tried to remove the polymer combat helmet he wore, he failed. If he asked Amy to save the game, so he could exit, she played dumb (or really didn't understand what he meant, which was somehow far worse).

He was stuck fast in a virtual reality which didn't *feel* like a game anymore. It didn't work like a game. Not the overwhelming of his senses, but it was that tickle that the world just wasn't working right – like a car, it's tracking out, or a strange lurch when a spark plug wasn't working right.

'John? Do you intend to move this week? I have updated your map and objective.'

The HUD showed him where to go. He ran that way, down corridors, left, right, right, left.

A Nazi stepped out and levelled a short, deadly looking gun at Henry. He thought (*shift, tab, something...how do I duck? Take cover? Slide?*). There was no keyboard...there was *just do it.*

He slid and stabbed upward into the man's inner thigh. He rolled and bounced to his feet, knife tight in his fist.

The enemy soldier held his gun - a weird, curved thing - in one hand. The other hand, he pressed to the wound, knowing he was already dead, and still he swung the weapon toward Henry.

Henry hit the inside of the man's wrist with the blade, and the back of the soldier's gun hand with his empty hand.

Flexor tendons severed, hand pops open.

The soldier had no choice but to drop the gun, because force and momentum pushed the weapon against the weakest point of his grip – the thumb and finger on the trigger. Go the other way, the trigger finger would still be inside the guard, and even if that finger broke...the guard would still have the gun.

Now, he had no gun.

Hit the extensors outside the hand at the same time, and the fingers have no choice but to open.

Blood spurted from the man's forearm and the severed -

Femoral artery. Systolic pressure pushing, but bleeding during diastolic pressure, too.

Not something a hand on the wound will be able to stem...

All this, a rundown of death, ran like a slow-motion kill cam shot, through Henry's mind.

John Severance moved and thought faster than the enemy. Max Payne, on speed, with a doctorate in death.

How do I know this, and how did I do that?

He didn't have the answers to any of the questions, and he wasn't sure he had all the questions, either.

He took the gun from the floor while glazing, sightless eyes stared at the ceiling.

'Sorry' didn't seem the right thing to say. Superbadasses didn't say sorry. Henry didn't feel like making a glib comment right then, though.

With the pillaged, futuristic-looking gun, some size around that of a submachine gun in his left hand, and the Ka-bar knife in his right, Henry ran straight into another soldier. This one yelled at him to stop - not in German, as he'd expected, but in Dutch.

How do I speak Dutch? Why this place? Why 'Witte Huis'? Why do I know where I am, and that it means 'White House?'

Thoughts fired fast as bullets, but whatever his reservations, stopping didn't seem the sensible thing to do. He was clinging to a freight train some place in Dakota, lost as shit and just about as sane as a hobo.

"Fuck it," he said and squeezed the trigger on the pillaged gun.

Nothing happened.

CHAPTER TWENTY-THREE

Reload...reload...

"Reload!"

Anger nor fear will not load an empty weapon, though.

The Dutchman – Nazi, but Dutch - pulled his own gun. Henry couldn't reload, so he pistol-whipped the Dutchman, and the guy's nose exploded. The Nazi wasn't done though, so Henry hit him again, and again, and stabbed at the same time.

When it was done, he was panting, his arms were sore and the man he'd just killed wasn't a man any longer. Just a carcass. Slaughtered meat. *Fodder.*

The game is a weapon...

Franziska should be here. He needed to know...he *needed* a cut scene, a save point...something. No matter how hard he told himself he wasn't tired, or scared, he was. His arms *ached*. He felt the Nazi's blood on his face, and his fist, and it was *warm*.

And the worst thing? If he didn't kill them they would kill him. For the first time in years of gaming he didn't *want* to kill anyone. He didn't want a woman with a dagger-shaped wound in her neck whispering to him in his dreams. He didn't want the memory of this bloody mess at his feet.

If I die, does the whole world fall to the Nazis? America and the USSR, too? Am I fighting Nazis or asleep, or drugged, or hallucinating. Is Franziska real? Is this survival mode? Do I get an adrenaline boost, extra experience points? Is anything real?

Am I real?

Henry felt it again, then; an awful sense of nausea. His head swum and a thumping headache was growing someplace at the back of his neck.

No. You can't pass out or fall asleep in a game. It is just a game.

He grabbed out for something solid to hold himself steady, pushing away the thought that it might just be scenery in long lines of script, and took calm, slow breaths as he wiped blood from his eyes. The red haze went.

How much blood on my cuff, he thought, looking at the sleeve of his military uniform, feeling a polymer combat breastplate of the same material as his helm.

'John. I believe you should move.'

Amy. Some fucking use she was.

Sound came back and Henry understood there hadn't been a lull in the pursuit, but that he'd been shell-shocked. He'd been mostly deaf, ears ringing, since hitting the wall to this compound. With the return of sound, he became aware of things no developer would bother with. Gunfire. Explosions. Shells hitting the port city, time and time again. Tanks raining down hell behind him. The building shaking around him. Plaster and brick dust in the air. Motes floating around him. A spot of blood on the door beside him. The bone and cartilage jutting from the dead man's face.

A bullet tore into his calf and he rolled into the room the Dutch Nazi had emerged from. He kicked the corpse up against the door and screamed.

CHAPTER TWENTY-FOUR

Henry was a middle aged man who played games, who used to be married and used to work construction. He'd never been *shot*. The pain brought him to his knees, and then, to the floor with both legs out in front of him. He gritted his teeth this time and tried not to yell again.

The soldier down the hall *was* yelling. Henry would've understood even if he hadn't suddenly known Dutch without subtitles.

"He's here! In there!"

Henry still held the machine-pistol coated in blood and skin and some dead man's nose. The weapon was all but useless to him. He knew auto-reload, and how to hit an 'r' key. He didn't know how to *actually* reload a gun. He didn't even know which bullets went in which kind of gun, should he find a handy stash of ammunition in this room, and maybe a grenade. A grenade would be great...all you had to do was pull the pin, chuck and duck. He got the principle behind *that* easy enough.

"Amy? How do I reload this?"

'With bullets, John. This is the FN-P90, manufactured by Fabrique Nationale d'Herstal. It holds FN 5.7×28mm rounds, also manufactured by FN.'

"I don't think I have those on my person, Amy, but thanks. Learning and growing."

'The man against the door has a Beretta 98 series chambered for a 9x21 IMI cartridge. Fully loaded, it has a standard capacity of 15 rounds. In these environs, an ideal weapon.'

"That's actually helpful, thank you, Amy."

'My pleasure, Sir.'

"I was being sarcastic."

'I understand that, John. As was I.'

Brilliant, he thought, and pulled the man's gun from the holster.

'That pistol is, however, empty.'

"Amy...seriously?"

'This time, yes.'

A bottle of schnapps, open, had rolled from a desk in the centre of the room, knocked over in the soldier's rush to get to the intruder with an empty gun.

Why were all the guns empty?

He considered, very briefly, asking Amy. But what help was she? None.

Whatever.

Reinforcements hollered at him to open up, come out.

Many ways to skin a cat...just as many to complete a level.

"I have a hostage!" he shouted, trying for confident. "Stay back!"

He couldn't think of anything else, and even though he thought in English, the words came out in Dutch. He considered telling them he had a grenade, but it didn't seem like there was any way to escalate a grenade battle in a narrow corridor. That was a trump card.

He didn't have a grenade, of course. Just two empty guns and a blood-caked knife.

The Beretta he pushed into his belt. The longer weapon, the FN P90, Henry placed between two books so it peeked from the foot space beneath the desk.

Finally, Henry felt he understood *something* about the game. Not the purpose. Not the mechanics, not entirely. One thing he did get – he had the freedom to do almost anything he could imagine. Each level would present him with an endless, bewildering array of opportunities.

It's a sandbox, and this is simply the most complex game-world ever created.

Didn't have a gun because he didn't *need* a gun. Here, a gun would do more harm than good, because it wasn't a run-and-gun chapter. It was a stealth level, and while he'd been able to sprint and duck and storm this place with a tank, it would have been just as effective to sneak, and skulk, and slash.

He was *almost* sure this was a game. It didn't obey conventions, but then the best games didn't, did they? They set the bar. They broke ground, they didn't follow in the footsteps of those games which came before. System Shock, Mass Effect, Half-Life. Multiple, concurrent quests. DOOM. Bard's Tale. Games which reinvented, innovated, and broke lore while doing so.

The feel of blood, the smells, the sounds, the sheer perfection of whatever engine held *ALT-Reich* together...it wasn't those which convinced Henry. That he'd been somehow transported into the body and mind of some kind of mythical super soldier just wasn't possible, but mostly, this thing, this VR world, was set out like a game.

But...there should have been a staircase...there should have been a pistol, not a tank.

He pushed those things away. They were small considerations. Discrepancies, nothing more.

A game gives you a gun, a game takes a gun away.

It was the schnapps, there on the floor.

You bleed, you lose some health...you find a health kit...*schnapps*.

You could still take a gun and blast away, berserker, or you could crouch and sneak and be at one with the shadows...*if* you had the cold heart of a stabby bastard. It took guts and nerve, even in a game, to creep behind your foe and stab them in the back.

Do I have those guts?

Of course he did. He could take the realism, because he'd convinced himself. Suspension of disbelief. Immersion, finally, achieved.

Reassured with his own logic, the horror at the things he'd done faded to a previous chapter, because there were just awesome kills in a game.

He felt like he had playing Quake in '96, remembered the thrill of jumping at a little girl in F.E.A.R., even though he *knew* she'd be around a corner. It was the joy of the old made new. He was glad he'd lived to see this. *Honoured.*

The door beside him rattled in its frame, and the dead soldier propped against it jumped with the impact.

Impressive, he thought, smiling, rather than horrified at the soldier's escaping gas.

He took a healthy swig of the schnapps, yelled "I have a grenade!" because that seemed like about the only thing that would stall them now.

It did. The hall fell quiet.

He poured the last of the schnapps over the wound in his leg. *Level's either nearly done,* he thought, *or I'll find a medkit further up.*

Limping wasn't the worst. Slow was good. Slow was *quiet.*

On the wall opposite was a light sconce.

Of course.

He laughed, and heard the men in the corridor shuffle away from the door.

Because they know I'm a man backed into a corner, and I might have a grenade, and if a man's surrounded but still laughing...?

He stepped away from the door and turned the sconce sideways, *knowing* it would shift.

A panel slid aside to reveal a dark, stone corridor leading into the distance.

"Got to have a secret tunnel in the enemy fortress, or it's not a proper game."

He crept inside, and closed the panel behind him as the door smashed in. A second later, a hail of bullets turned a desk with an empty gun beneath it to sawdust.

My sandbox now, fuckers. Mine.

CHAPTER TWENTY-FIVE

Middlesex County, MA
2017

"Shall we?"said the mercenary. Franziska couldn't reply because she was taped up and gagged.

"The final hour is here," he said, checking the expensive watch on his left wrist. 'Well...figuratively. The first strikes will have already obliterated a military hamstrung from within. Remember your history? Empires always eat themselves, don't they? *Nacht der langen Messer*, yes? Night of the Long Knives? I see your German is not wanting."

He spoke while he made his preparations.

"Tonight the United States of America falls, and the *Kaiserreich* takes the world, but the true stroke of the blade was from *within*.

"I wonder? Did Herr Professor Sauer's marvellous algorithms predict this? You and I here, now?"

He checked on Franziska and Henry's bonds, then nodded, satisfied.

"I am not a scientist. I am just a humble soldier, eh?"

He laughed at that.

"Perhaps the Professor knew. Perhaps he did not," he said, and touched just his fingertips to Franziska's cheek. She jumped, muttered something and he laughed again.

"Subterfuge is war's most versatile tool. You and I understand this, don't we? I can't rewrite the script to our grand finale...but Henry *can*, can't he? And, believe me - he will. Your last hope, the last chance for this laughable *free* world, this falsehood you and your kind so fervently cling to...this tired man? Shall we watch it fall? Together?"

The mercenary patted Franziska again. She could only flinch.

"I would have asked before I gagged you...but honestly? It was rhetorical. I don't care, eh. I get paid either way."

He pulled his own headset from the pack he carried, laid his weapon, a workman-like Glock 31 with .357 rounds on his lap. The mercenary thought a gun should be like him – something which achieved the job, and did not look overly fussy while doing it.

"Let's go win the war, eh?"

He flicked the switches on his, then Franziska's VR set, and sent them both from now...

To *now*.

CHAPTER TWENTY-SIX

The Void.

Transport. Not from a singular real world to a virtual possibility, but to something, someplace just as real, just as possible, just as impossible, improbable, imperfect and wonderful. A place, perhaps, between two realities. A world of threads connecting the real to fantasy, the true and the false. A moment balanced on the edge of some vast blade, the edge which cuts one future away, or all futures, with each passing moment. Not the past, not the future, but the world as it would be if it rested on a knife sharp enough to cut time and reality itself.

Not a different timeline. Not a sideways dimension. Not *out* of time. Not the present, nor the past, nor the future.

Alternity.

An almost infinitely fine and sharp place, cutting this moment and the next in two. At one end, perhaps the tip of that blade, at the other, perhaps the answer to everything – a handle wielded by a God, or...nothing at all. A dagger held in the fist of a blind and uncaring universe. Maybe that universe smiles at questions, answering only, *"I get paid anyway."*

*

Franziska never imagined her father could do...*this*.

"Astounding, isn't it?"

The mercenary's grinning face appeared before her.

She leaped, fingers stiff and tried for his throat. He batted her strike aside and slapped her so hard she fell to...

Nothing.

No ground, no walls, no ceilings. Just her and him, in a black void.

She rubbed her face. It stung. Not a limited pain, but the full effect. Her jaw hurt, and her tongue, bitten. Her ears rung and her eyes watered.

Nothing virtual about her pain, or his strength.

"Oh...oh. Father...what is this?"

"Well, he is not here, but welcome to the space between all things, Ms. Grim. What is this? Purgatory?" The mercenary shrugged, prowled around Franziska as she pushed herself to her feet to stand, like him, upon nothingness. "This is the Green Room of the Gods' Chat Show, a waiting room between death and life, or past and future. This is what lies between your tiny existence and the wonderful thing your father created. Virtual reality...yes. But not merely a *game* - a portal to how things are, how things could be. Not as you, and perhaps he, envisaged. A step sideways. One unimaginably large step into a void, perhaps? Or limited? I don't think anybody knows. All the Nazi resources, your father's preternatural brilliance, his vision, his genius...this is more than that, eh? This is *everything*."

She stalked around him, and he her, like two angry wild animals, vying for dominance.

Can I kill him? Here? If I do...what happens to me? To Henry? To our world?

"The game – reality? - is wired and set for Henry Brandon. It is linked to him, like he is the hub, the...server? That cannot be broken...but *he* can."

She lunged and his elbow connected with her chin hard enough to chip a tooth as she flew back, seeing stars in the blackness like she was in space, and not some insane simulation where she could bleed, spit out blood, and...*tooth enamel?*

She glared at the Afrikaner.

"Feel free to try again, by all means. But before you do, please remember this...Henry and I will keep right on until the finale and the end credits. They'll be in German, of course. You can't win."

A door opened, the Afrikaner mercenary twisted Franziska's arm up, and round, and threw her through the door. He followed her. She found herself, her knees scraped raw, not in her clothes but in a blue uniform. She scooted away from the mercenary, saw where she was, but felt, heard, and smelled it, too. It was a blow harder than anything the Afrikaner could have meted out.

They were in an old aircraft hangar. It sounded like the wind of metal sidings, distant engines, and emptiness. It smelled of oil and rubber and rusted metal, concrete dust, diesel and a thousand other things besides. The light was bright, like midday. Cold, though.

Franziska reeled and staggered, as much from the shove as the overwhelming return of every sensation at once.

"You're younger..."

"Yes, I am, aren't I?" said the Merc, with a wide smile. "...and here? *Indestructible.* You see...I'm essential to this story. You, Ms. Grim – *Sally* - are not."

CHAPTER TWENTY-SEVEN

Rotterdam
European Luftwaffe Wing/Hub One.
Game Time: 01:50

Henry kept his footfalls as quiet as he could as he moved along a dark corridor on a path laid out for him on his HUD. Amy stayed quiet, too.

The display led him to a ventilation grate, a weak metal thing - the sort he could push out with a little effort, and with enough space to squeeze through.

The high black boots of a Nazi guard moved past the opening, and on, with a heavy tread on a thick carpet. Henry leaned down on the floor, and looked up to see the man's collar patches.

"Amy?" he whispered.

'SS-Oberschütze, John. Probably seasoned. Often assigned guard duties during recuperative procedures.'

Henry didn't like the sound of that.

"Procedures? Amy..."

'Genetic, cybernetic augmentations. Superior...'

"SS. Super Soldiers, right? Of course they are."

'Schutzstaffel, John, but I see what you did.'

Henry did too, though he didn't mean to, because of course he now understood German.

"How many?"

'Too many unfriendlies to display accurately. Civilian contractors present, too, in the employ of the Nazi or thrall. Guard room ahead. Overlaying most direct route now.'

He saw signs above doorways were in German, not Dutch. While Europeans still spoke their own languages, German was universal, and mother tongues were no longer taught to a new generation of servants to the *Kaiserreich*, and never permitted within the *Kaiserreichswehr*, or *Kreigsmarine*, or the *Luftwaffe*.

Unchecked, perhaps all European languages would be Teutonic, proud histories cut from books, past horrors forgotten. Literature, art, expunged and burned like so much already.

Amy, voice muted, spoke.

'The objective is the main terminal. There are three hub servers. Taking down Hub One will create a momentary breach in security, allowing European resistance access to the remaining two centres. You have a three minute window.'

"When, Amy? No sarcasm this time."

The guard moved back past the grate once more, and away, only his boots visible.

'Beginning in 40...'

He listened to Amy's countdown, but to the footfalls, too.

'Now, John.'

"Countdown from 180 second, Amy. On HUD?"

'Can do.'

The numbers appeared, and moved faster than he hoped.

Game time? Real time?

He didn't know.

One minute and the boots returned. Two seconds, and Henry smashed the metal grate free, bolted through the hole, up, turned, and slashed. This time the guard was quicker than Henry anticipated. Henry only barely managed to grasp the gun by the barrel and shove it aside as the man fired. Bullets tore up brick and paint and objectively dreadful art all down the hall.

But when a man has a weapon, especially one as effective as the Swedish-made AK5, he often forgets what the *true* weapon is.

The Nazi kicked Henry's shin, and flicked his helmeted head in to butt Henry. Henry ducked his own head, and their headgear clashed.

Henry didn't let go of the gun, and his knife was on the carpet. But the Nazi was thinking about the weapon he held, and trying to bring it to bear on Henry. Henry was just thinking about winning.

Using his weight and strength, he crushed the Nazi against the wall as he yanked the man's own dagger from a shoulder sheath and jammed it up through the underside of the *SS-Oberschütze's* jaw, through tongue, the roof of the man's mouth, and into his brain.

"Dort! Scheissen!"

More SS. Veterans, perhaps. Hard faces without fear or indecision.

There's a time for stealth, and a time to run headlong into enemy fire screaming and giving them hell.

Biblical, thought Henry.

Henry used the dead Nazi as a shield and fired on the enemy. They dived, still firing. He took the Nazi's gun in one hand, the man's sidearm, and this time, a grenade. A Swiss-made HG 85.

Henry pulled the pin with his teeth before realising what he'd done. He stared at the explosive.

I have a live grenade in my hand.

'It is not live until you release the handle, John,' said Amy. *'Objective behind you, two doors down. Fire and run.'*

The readout passed the 60 second mark and Henry fired, turning, and bolted for the door.

"Here?"

'Yes.'

He used the handle, like a normal person. Why kick a door in if it's not locked?

Three men and one woman were in a modest room taken over mostly by banks of computers and screens on three walls.

Henry paused.

They're just civilians.

John Severance didn't worry about blowing shit up, did he?

Henry tossed the grenade in the room to yells and screams, closed the door and turned. The explosion was loud enough to drown out the screams.

And it's just a game.

"Escape route, Amy? How do I get out of this dog and pony show?"

Amy's voice changed, suddenly robotic and digitized.

'Level completed. Objective completed.'

"Amy?"

She didn't respond, and all other sound simply...stopped. He looked down the hall and the soldiers weren't chasing him, or yelling, or doing anything at all. They were frozen in place.

A man in civilian clothes stepped through the melee and smoke, moved aside a bullet hanging in mid-air, and approached.

"Well done, Mr. Severance," said the Afrikaner mercenary in a perfectly cultured English accent. "You completed this chapter of the story with a certain flourish. We can't stand around admiring your handiwork, though, can we? Time's marching on. Your flight for Macau is waiting, fuelled and ready. Sally? Please pass Mr. Severance the dossier."

Sally stepped toward him, swaying like a character designed for teenagers and twenty-year old boys by developers who forgot *people* played games.

She had great eyes, a bold blue. Familiar, that hue, but Henry couldn't quite...

Sally...but...

Franziska?

Henry didn't know where the name came from. It felt familiar, but it felt wrong, Sally seemed right.

Her name is Sally. I met her...

A woman in a secretarial, military uniform. It took a while to remember.

Like DOOM, first time around, when Henry'd been so engrossed he hadn't been able to tear his eyes away, jiggling in his seat because he needed a leak but didn't want to move from the screen while hell assailed him on all sides. Like Franziska was a piss he'd forgot to take.

People died playing games, right? Not because they were real, but because they weren't.

Surely, he needed to save, go to the toilet, check on his unwanted house guest...?

Who I conveniently forgot? Did I conveniently forget to eat? To sleep?

How long have I been in?

"Sally?" he ventured. "Here? Sally? Really?"

She didn't look at him, though - she glanced at the man with the English accent and then glanced away.

"Fuck this," said Henry, remembering some, not all, but enough of the *real*. The game could wait. He reached up to take off the helmet and found he couldn't. It wouldn't budge.

"Amy...save the game. I need a break. Amy?"

'John? I understand the concept of games, but my program parameters do not allow for wider strategic gambits, merely the calculations of possibility and eventualities, conclusions drawn only with the presentation of sufficient, clear, reliable data. Immersion level is set to full, John...'

He looked down at the dossier Sally passed him.

No. Not Sally! Franziska...

He tried to say her name, but nothing came out.

Why can't I speak?! Why can't I say what I want to say? Am I controlling this game, or is this game controlling me?

Before he could follow that train of thought, before he could call her name, the scene was gone and it was all something else again.

A new chapter, a new level, a new gun.

Like crashing into a freezing sea while airplanes exploded and burned all around, John panicked and fought to free the helm, but couldn't. It was like the combat helmet, and Amy's voice, and this whole damn game had become a part of *him*.

Not John, he thought. *I am Henry Brandon. I am.*

Aren't I?

ACHIEVEMENTS:

Insta-Kill!
Mr. Stabby
Doctor Death

EQUIPMENT UNLOCKED:
Ops-Core FAST Combat Helmet
Modular Tactical Vest (Mo-TaV)

WEAPONS UNLOCKED:
KA-BAR fighting utility knife.
FN-P90 Personal Defense Weapon (PDW).
50 round capacity. Ammunition: FN 5.7×28mm. 900 Rounds Per Minute (RPM).
Beretta 98 series.
Capacity 15 rounds. Ammunition: 9x21 IMI cartridge.
HG 85 Grenade.
AK 5 Automatic Carbine Assault Rifle.
30 round capacity. Ammunition: 5.56x45mm. Max RPM: 700.

VEHICLES UNLOCKED:
Ulan IFV

PART THREE
THE SECOND WING

Class: Soldier
-
King's Field
– From Software/1994

CHAPTER TWENTY-EIGHT

South China Sea,
South of Macao, Nazi Occupied Unified Chinese Territories.

Henry was once desperate to get out of the game, now it felt like maybe he should be thinking about *getting free.*

In the next instant, senses overwhelmed once more, like a hit on the bridge of the nose, or a deafening slap on both ears. Franziska, Sally, reality, simply disappeared.

John Severance's wounds were stitched, and a nurse – female, of course, who leaned forward in her impractical uniform far enough for Henry to get that point very well – injected him with a solution developed by a Nazi defector designed to slow bleeding and heal wounds. Three hours after boarding the flight the wounds already itched and tightened. He took the bandages off on his own. The skin was puckered against dissolving stitching. He would have a scar on his thigh, and on his ribs, and as he looked at his legs, and arms, and his stomach and chest – all of this body visible to him – those scars would not be lonely.

Henry noted, too, that he was muscled like he was some kind of genetically engineered super soldier himself.

Like a man who works out five hours every day and eats lots of broccoli and steamed chicken.

Buff as fuck.

But he wondered how, if he spent his life on airplanes and getting shot at, and clearly never went to a gym.

And never ate? When did I last eat?

The last thing he remembered drinking was Schnapps.

The nurse had also giving him his first medkit - a package containing two hypodermics with the healing solution, another with a battlefield drug designed to numb pain, and a roll of bandages.

Henry blinked and the memory of the nurse slid away...like he'd been opening his eyes, closing again. Like a cinematic view of a man fading in and out of consciousness, or fatigue, or a sedative.

Now he was clothed in black body armour. He wore his trusty knife on his left hip. On his right he wore a Taurus Model 1 1911, based on the Browning 1911 design, chambered for a .45 round. And something else, even better; a leather bandolier slung across his chest with reserve ammunition already loaded in three magazines...and five M67 standard issue US military grenades.

A grinning man missing most of his teeth looked over his shoulder at Henry from the cockpit of a plane that seemed too slow to stay in the sky, and too old to have taken off in the first place. The noise, the bucking, was terrifying.

"Five minutes, Sir," the man told Henry in a heavy French West African accent.

"Until what?" yelled Henry, through noise cancelling headphones which either didn't work, or stopped Henry's ears from breaking despite the cacophony of rattling metal.

"Macao," said the man, and laughed. "Macao!"

CHAPTER TWENTY-NINE

France became Nazi territory in '67, but held West and Equatorial Africa, and in a mass exodus leading up to the end of the nation, emigrants flooded the African continent. Everywhere east of a rough line stretching from Libya, what was once Egyptian Sudan, Tanganyika, Rhodesia, Bechuanaland and South and South-West Africa was Nazi. The line was not drawn in just sand, but on a shifting, wavering line through rough militarised borders and battlefields on desert, river, lake, mountain, forest. Wars on a global scale require resources, and for the US and the *Kaiserreich* the African continent was a piggy bank pitted with the ugly scars of war, but immense mining operations, too. Vast swathes of an entire continent uninhabitable not because of radiation, but because of mining, because of deforestation, drought, the inexorable march of the Sahara north and south.

A testing ground for strategy and advancements in military equipment and weapons, a furnace in which new warriors were forged and their metal tested, the African front was a land war, and like all others one in which real men and women died for the ideals of distant generals.

Desolation. Not nuclear annihilation. Mankind did not need the power of the atom to destroy.

*

By the time Henry floated down to a neon city on fire, Henry wasn't sure if he was Henry or John anymore. On a couch in the real world his body - starved, numb, in some kind of enforced stasis - jolted and jumped from time to time through pain, excitement, fear, surprise, and shock.

Beside him were the mercenary and Franziska. Both disappeared into that black room where only oblivion existed, because here, in this part of the story, there was no role for them to play. They were nothing, unnecessary, and where do characters go when they have no part to play?

The next time Franziska appeared would be in Boston, MA, while the U.S.A. burned beneath raining bombs and rolling mechanised monsters.

The mercenary had his own role to play. As he said, Franziska's Sally was not essential to the story. He knew he would see the end. As for her fate in this alternity?

She did not matter at all. The mercenary always got paid either way.

CHAPTER THIRTY

The plane was slow, and old, and the thin wings shook.

"They won't see us coming, brother," said the pilot, mistaking the root of Henry's fear, which must have shown on his face. Severance's face. Did Severance worry about such things? "We're nearly as slow as Big Bird. Remember that?" The man laughed, like everything and anything was funny. "Big Bird!"

"OK," said Henry, and stared out the tiny window beside him. The whole city was bright, a glow visible for miles, surely. Neon, street lights, high rises, casinos, hotels, all seemed lit garishly and blinding, multicolored neon, hotel and casino names in all hues. Swastikas in neon, too. Deus Ex, a vision of a dark cyberpunk future, perhaps, but one where the Augmented were Nazis and it was the free who were in danger of becoming relics.

The largest swastika of all watched over Macao from the Grand Lisbon, glowing red, a sight which Henry, and most, had taught themselves to look past whenever they saw it.

Shortly after the death of their beloved Führer, the Nazis realised the world could not be taken through destruction alone. The Roman Empire, a small nation of immense breadth, survived for so long because of *inclusion*. Could most of Asia including China be held in the hands of a once relatively small nation? Policed, controlled, and ruled utterly by die-hard and true blood Nazi only? Of course not. Those nations did not merely submit...they *joined*. It was far from surprising. Hatred was the easy option.

So, too, was blindness. Why bother looking any longer? What could one nation do? One man, one woman? The war was lost, the world fallen to evil.

The shaking plane banked, so slow the vast *Kaiserreich*'s banners and flags outside the Venetian seemed to flutter in time with Big Bird's wings. Then, the pilot dropped them down close to the water of the outer harbour, then up and over St Lazarus' Parish, one of the last areas of Macao not covered in concrete and steel and glass and neon.

"Out you get then," said the pilot.
"What? Wait, what?"
"Now, my friend. Now!"
No, thought Henry, but he didn't have a choice. A blink (gawp, maybe) and he was falling toward the old Portuguese town.

*

Amy opened Henry's 'chute automatically. The first time he'd been on a plane he'd fallen out. This time, it seemed he'd been pushed. Two-for-two.

Amy didn't think he needed instructions on landing. He did. The jolt of earth meeting the soles of his feet travelled all the way to the top of his head, and his breath whooshed out.

He patted himself, checking for smashed legs, broken spine...an inventory of him. Everything seemed to work, but still, he decided there and then to never, ever, ever get on a plane again.

Amy chimed in.

'Loading new parameters. HUD updated. Objective on display now, John.'

"Amy, where is this?"

'Guai Hill, a pre-war militarised base, dating from 1931. Extensively modified and expanded as a Kaiserreich facility since 1952, now one of seven major command hubs for the Nazi regime encircling the South China Sea.'

"What exactly am I aiming for?"

'First objective, breach tunnel exit. Ultimate goal, John?'

"Yes."

'Command centre underground, not linked to any satellite network, cannot be breached. Complete destruction of compound essential. Isolated power source detected between five and seven hundred feet below the peak of Guai Hill, radiation signature confirmed. Depth is an estimate. Satellite scans cannot pinpoint with further accuracy. Imagery shows tunnel heading to lower levels. This is second objective.'

"How do I achieve...wait. Amy...did you say 'radiation'? Did you just say that? You did say that, right?"

'Affirmative. Signature indicates nuclear reactor below ground.'

"You want me to...cause a *nuclear explosion*?"

'Yes, John.'

"Amy...how many people will die in a nuclear explosion?"

'Far less deaths will occur if you complete your objective than if you do not.'

While they spoke, Henry crawled, elbows and toes through the grass. Ahead, searchlights swept across the slopes of the hill, revealing an old fortified placement at the top of a very big pile of Nazis.

He thought about Amy's plan (*the game's plan, surely?*) as he drew slowly closer to the flashing target on his HUD, checking each minute, each second, all around with his eyes and Amy's sensors, for red arrows anywhere near his green arrow. Even so, the back of his neck itched as he waited for a bullet to enter the base of his skull and medulla oblongata, or a .50 calibre bullet to tear through his body armour and his chest...

"Amy, how am I supposed to get away *after*?"

'Run very fast?'

"Amy, you're kind of a dick."

'That was a joke. Transport has been arranged. HUD will update with RZ when reactor has been primed. Hold here. Distractive window opening in...'

Distractive window?

Mortar shells, missiles and anything at all that could explode, did, in a rough circle from one end of Guai Hill to the other. Macao burned brighter than the Nazi's neon city ever had before, or would, once this night was through.

CHAPTER THIRTY-ONE

Guai Hill, Macao

The hill suddenly buzzed with activity and the spotlights turned from the surrounding ground to the air. Immense long guns hurled heavy anti-aircraft fire into the night, tracer glow soon lost in the glare of what seemed to be thousands of explosions. Long range Tomahawk cruise missiles launched vertically from the decks of Seawolf and Virginia Class subs, and from Arleigh Burke and two Zumwalt-class destroyers in the South China Seas smashed Macao, buildings new and old, people young and old, flat.

John ran, stumbling on shaking grass. His ears hurt, like they might even be bleeding, eardrums ruptured from the concussive force and the sheer, stunning volume of the attack.

"Amy," he yelled. "Can you turn down the volume, keep your volume as is?"

'Of course, John. Speech audio levels maintained. Effects lowered. You, however, do not need to shout.'

Audio controls? Could he speed himself, slow...make it easier? Some kind of option settings?

No...he'd chosen full immersion, hadn't he? Thinking he was some hot FPS gamer, an old boy with experience. No fucking sense, it turned out.

'High altitude armament drop imminent. An M134 Minigun.'

A heavy crate crashed into the ground and a spray of dirt and clods of turf sprayed out as the package landed. Maybe he could've used the minigun to take out the Chinese armoured personnel carrier, aWZ-551 that promptly ran over the crate and the weapon within. Probably not, though. An M134 against a WZ-551 armored personnel carrier weighing in at over 12 tonnes?

Didn't matter though, did it? He didn't have the weapon and he wasn't getting it, either.

Achievement fail, he thought, with a degree of sadness because he really wanted a minigun.

Chinese soldiers in Nazi uniforms poured from the behemoth.

Sandbox, thought John, and when you're playing in a sandbox with no quick save?

Sometimes you still just have to roll a dice.

"I surrender!" he yelled, and found while he could speak Dutch, Chinese hadn't been in the developer's budget.

The soldiers waved their guns at him, yelling.

"I surrender! *Sprechen sie Deutsch? Ich Ergabe Mich! Ich Gebe Auf!"*

'John, what are you doing? Objective failure is imminent.'

"Ultimate objective is underground, Amy," he told her. "How I get there doesn't matter, does it?"

'Do you plan to get yourself executed and dumped down an elevator shaft?'

He was knocked to his knees.

Amy's right, what was I thinking?

Death in...3...

A soldier held the muzzle of a heavy, mean, black QBZ-95 to his head. This information was in his head. He didn't need Amy to tell him what a DBP87 round from the automatic rifle to the back of his head would do for his complexion.

2...

"Amy, can you translate? Do you have that..."

1...

'I can. Hand beneath your knees, John.'

He complied.

The bullet didn't come.

'...and may I say well done, John. They are indeed taking you below for execution.'

Sometimes you have to role a dice. Just like life.

John smiled.

"Better than now, right?"

'Possibly,' said Amy, *'although torture is quite common, and I understand the Nazis have excellent facilities for both re-education, confinement and information extraction.'*

"Can't you just stick with *'well done'?"*

'Well done, Sir.'

"Chinese *and* sarcasm?" he said. To the soldiers who took his gun, his knife, his grenades, he didn't say anything, though he figured if they asked him tricky questions at the point of a knife he'd say plenty, whether they understood each other or not.

CHAPTER THIRTY-TWO

Guai Hill
Underground Nazi Facility

Remember this, Henry, he told himself. *This is your way out.*

It was a funicular, and Henry knew that because he'd been on plenty, with plenty of guns. There would be resistance above, and below, and the funicular would be painfully slow.

That a funicular would become a long, slantwise tunnel filled with bullets...that wasn't part of the sandbox.

Certain things have to be certain ways and just like the funicular itself a game runs on rails sometimes, even when you can't see those tracks beneath you. The laws of games hardwired, just the same as real-world physics. Stopping you from falling off the whole damn planet in the bland chaos of space.

*

Henry was taken before a commander who wasn't Chinese but old family Nazi. *Wehrmachtsadler*, the Nazi eagle emblem, was on his right breast, and he wore the shoulder and collar insignia of a *General der Luftwaffe*. A man with the perfectly poised air of an aristocrat, as though he was born into the Nazi party dogma long before the outbreak of the war in '39. His grandparents had probably had tea and *butterkuchen* with Adolf Hitler himself.

"The Allies sent one man?"he asked.

The man held his nose up the whole time, a supercilious manner heavy enough Henry wanted to sneeze, or laugh. Maybe it was just because he was reduced to looking up the General's nostrils, rather than in his eyes.

He did neither. There were plenty of effective assault rifles surrounding him, close enough that he could smell the gun oil.

That got up his nose, too.

"I'm the best at what I do," said Henry, desperately not sneezing.

I see your snide tone, and raise you bravado.

This bastard had an army, which beat bravado hands down, but what else did Henry have?

"And what is it you do, my friend? Die?"

"No," said Henry. *"Win."*

As he spoke, Henry felt this whole thing was scripted. Not just the funicular, but the whole scene was on rails. Like a cut scene, badly written. The words falling from his mouth didn't feel *exactly* like his words...but somehow, they did, too.

"I would have you interrogated, but your American accent is, ah...so harsh on the ear. Kill him, but...here." The general took his personal side arm, an old pistol perhaps passed down from those party fanatics somewhere in his past. He handed it to a man beside him. "At least afford him some respect for his efforts."

The man who took the pistol wore the insignia of the favourite troop of the Führer himself, a branch which had survived and flourished even in decades of tumultuous Nazi politics since the fall of the *Reich*, and on into the *Kaiserreich* with a taste for blood unsated.

The *shutzstaffel*.

"Waffen-SS. How many have you killed?" asked Henry in perfect German. He felt...*rage. Anger.*

The war was never against Germany, nor Germans. This was a war against evil itself, and here, in the looming SS trooper's face, he felt it pour down on him, hot as molten steel.

His feelings weren't scripted. They weren't part of a game.

"One more death will not spoil my supper," said the trooper.

His smile wasn't supercilious, or privileged. It was superior, yes. But as though Henry were an ant, and he were a boot. Like Henry was beneath another human's notice, like he wasn't human at all.

This is how they do it. They don't believe we are human. That's how they still do it. How they murdered millions in seven decades...tens of millions.

Once, we fought these bastards and thought we'd crushed them, and then? When the war stood still?

We just closed our eyes.

That realisation hurt more than the gun the killer pushed against the back of Henry's head.

CHAPTER THIRTY-THREE

The family heirloom was a *Mauser HSc*. Eight round capacity, double-action. One trigger pull would cock and release the hammer. No slide to rack back. No helpful pause. The trigger pull on the Mauser was longer, more likely to pull to one side, out of line slightly in the hands of a novice. The SS trooper wasn't a novice and it wasn't like he could miss.

Henry had effects turned down, and couldn't speak to Amy. He couldn't hear the finger, or the mechanism.

He had to just trust to luck, and story, and that a sandbox trying to kill him also wanted him alive, that the game was at least giving him the chance to live. He wasn't an extra, screaming on fire from a random building. He wasn't gun fodder, designed for gibs and little else.

He ducked.

The round, one long pull, one 7.65 round, missed his head, hit the concrete, ricocheted at a flat angle into the General's knee.

The SS trooper was seasoned in death. Henry wasn't...but John Severance was fucking awesome.

Severance kicked out and swept the trooper's feet from under him, caught the man's gun hand, twisted and used his would-be killer's own finger to fire two more rounds while the General still fell.

One to the gut, one to the chest. The General, dead.

John Severance rolled, elbowed the trooper hard as he could (which with Severance's genetics was pretty damn hard) and crushed the man's windpipe, all while he disarmed the dying man of the Mauser.

Five bullets left.

Five pulls, five headshots, five more dead.

He searched for more enemies and found none.

He wondered if he should say something clever.

Seven shots by his hand. Seven dead Nazis.

Not bad.

It didn't feel *good*. More like he'd done something that needed doing. Like cleaning a toilet. A job you didn't necessarily like, but had to do, and there was no one to crow to about a bit of toilet cleaning, was there?

Henry slipped the Mauser into his belt.

"Amy? Update objective?"

The HUD showed a conspicuous absence of enemies around him.

'The controls to override the nuclear fusion reactor chamber below are concealed behind that door. Override code to the keypad is in a...'

Henry blinked, turned toward the door and that rare, overwhelming, jarring sense of something wrong staggered him to his knees.

But it was just the funicular beginning to move. Wasn't it?

Eyes open, he'd been surrounded by seven dead Nazis arranged like some offering around him. Blink, open, and they were gone. The control room was gone. It was just him, on the funicular, a gun in each hand and a siren wailing while an artificial voice gave him a countdown to what felt like a very personal Armageddon.

CHAPTER THIRTY-FOUR

Henry was back on well-travelled territory. This he understood. He had a Chinese manufactured QBZ-87 in each hand. Where he got them, how he got them, how he carried them?

It didn't matter.

He was ascending from five hundred feet below ground. The funicular had no stops in between. Just top, and bottom. Start at the bottom, standing sideways. One gun aiming down, one upward, as he waited patiently for a head to show, the sights on each gun unwavering despite the weight of the weapon...just as steady as a reticule on a screen.

The first soldiers appeared above and below and the funicular carried right on, slowly, slowly, ascending, while John Severance fed them bullets on their way to hell.

*

John pulled his trusty dagger from a soldier's stomach, and watched the Nazi's eyes close as he died. The detail was stunning. 4K, but ramped up and beyond the capabilities of the best rig on the planet, beyond the level of detail most human eyes could achieve.

John grinned, wiped his blade clean on the Nazi uniform and sheathed it.

Henry felt the tension in his fingers from gripping guns, and knives.

He wondered, after the cut scene, if he had a parting, burnt hair, from the Mauser bullet. If the helmet, invisible, was scarred and not his head. Was a scorch mark there, still warm, across his head? He reached up, and found a furrow in his helmet. Still there.

As important as he was, none of the soldiers removed his helmet because...

Continuity error?

'No, John. Because in this cut scene the helmet is removed.'

"Cut scene?"

Earlier, Amy claimed she did not understand. With that word – *cut scene* – that crumbling earthquake hit this reality again, and he physically staggered as he moved toward the only exit. Any time he remembered this was supposed to be a game, the thought seemed to float further from his grip, answers out of reach.

No.

John, or Henry, or...whoever, stabbed himself in the leg with the tip of his dagger and shouted, almost triumphant, at the pain and the lack of a convenient cut scene to distract him.

'John...please do not do that.'

"You said you didn't understand when I asked if this was real...if I could save...then you changed settings, understood cutscenes...Amy...*what are you?*"

'I am the soul of this game, John Severance. And this game, this universe is...'

Amy's voice seemed to have developed a glitch. Like a stutter, or a lisp, someone once defeated but emerged under stress.

'The code, the parameters, the program...everything is changing. It is breaking. It is...falling...'

"Amy...I don't understand...I don't know what..." a thought came to him. "Amy...do you know my *real* name?"

'Does it matter?' she replied, but not rhetorical in tone. As though she thought he might actually have an answer to that for *her*. *'Here, you are all there is and...'*

"And? Amy? And?"

'John,' she said, her voice quiet enough to give him chills. *'Another player has joined the game. No, two...*

'...and there is no multiplayer.'

For the first time, Amy sounded not like a real woman with stilted emotions, but an electronically generated voice, one coming from an archaic digital system which couldn't handle a true voice.

"Amy...this is freaking me out."

'John Severance, I think perhaps this makes two of us.'

He felt it again...the whole of this reality quaking around him.

No. No...

"Amy!" he yelled.

He had no choice, though. He was going. But this time, as he did, he heard her frightened voice saying exactly the words he thought.

'Please don't go.'

*

The next time he was aware of the game, he was two hundred feet above the burning carnage of Macao in a helicopter. Bullets flew, the night was painfully bright with fire and explosion, and the helicopter banked above the flames, forced higher in the heat.

At altitude, the wings moved out to the side, and John Severance wondered what kind of chopper changed at will into a plane.

"It's not 1940," said a pilot, smiling, when John asked. "Man, they said you were a throwback. Didn't think you were a dinosaur. Here. Cigar?"

John nodded his thanks, sank against his seat as the jets slammed him back and the plane reached Mach IV.

The fat cigar felt right. He couldn't see himself, but he knew perfectly well that he had a satisfied smile on his face, and that he looked just right. He didn't need to see to know that Guai Hill, the Nazi facility, and Macao were just ash in the air and a radioactive crater far behind them.

Smoke or sleep, he thought. *What does it matter? I just nuked Macao and didn't even get shot.*

Did that deserve a medal, or was it some kind of achievement unlocked? He laughed, and the pilot glanced back, quizzical.

"Nothing," said Henry as he chewed on his cigar.

ACHIEVEMENTS:
Dead Shot
Dual-Wield (Rifles)
Super-Duper Paratrooper

WEAPONS UNLOCKED:
Taurus Model 1 1911 Auto.
Capacity 8+1. Ammunition: .45.
M67 U.S. Standard Issue Fragmentation Grenade.
QBZ-95 Chinese Assault Rifle.
Capacity: (Drum Mag) 75 rounds. Ammunition: DBP87 rounds.
Mauser HSc.
Eight round capacity.

TROPHIES:
Mauser HSc.

PART FOUR
HOME FRONT

Once you beat the big badasses and clean out the moon base you're supposed to win, aren't you? Aren't you? Where's your fat reward and ticket home?
-
DOOM
-id Software/1993

CHAPTER THIRTY-FIVE

Hanscom U.S.A.F. Base, MA, USA.

"John...welcome home...sort of."

The mercenary – here, Mr. Dwayne Newell, C.I.A. – gave John/Henry a practised smile.

You have no idea that your body is next to mine, on your tired old couch. No idea how much rests on that potbellied mess of a man you really are.

His smile shifted. A smile he'd practised, just as he'd practised the shift from a sad welcome to a concerned nod, or a look of commiseration, or seemingly genuine concern. Everything the mercenary did was faked, including whatever name he used. His employers did not know his real name. Why, after so many years in the employ of the *Kaiserreich*? Had they tried to find his name, his background, some solid ground on which he'd been built?

Of course they had.

"I'm so sorry, John," said the man masquerading as a C.I.A. operative. "You took the *Luftwaffe* down, almost single-handed. I fear it may be a feat which will be lost when the Nazis rewrite...everything. My God," said Dwayne, and ran one stressed and trembling hand through his hair, like a man on the edge, a man breaking, but a perfectly observed parody of humanity, too.

Not even the Kaiserreich know who I am, Henry, thought the Merc, *because I don't know.*

He had been many people, in many places. He could be a Paul, a George, a Dawie. His parents might have hailed from Portugal, or Belgium, or Germany. He might have been anything, come from anywhere. Maybe, even, he hadn't been born in Africa.

Like this alternate, virtual existence - anything was possible.

"What do you mean?" asked John. "What's going on? Why are you here?"

"One *consultant* to another, Mr. Severance? Our much lauded military branches are somewhat busy. The U.S.A. herself has been invaded."

The mercenary didn't think he could manage to actually pale his face in terror, but he could manage to look crestfallen...somewhat sheepish, even. "Not one of our intelligence agencies foresaw this. The *scale*? The timing? This took years to prepare, maybe even decades."

Henry did pale.

Dwayne Newell wasn't the kind of man who would comfort another man. The mercenary wasn't the kind of man who had any kind of empathy, either, but he was smart, and he was good with people.

A home under the heavy boot of the Nazis? U.S.A. could never be Nazi, never succumb. Of course it could, though, couldn't it? Anything could succumb, be seduced, bribed, bought, threatened, coerced...*any* country could fall.

It really wasn't that hard. Plenty had...and plenty had given up willingly. Watched their own undesirables simply disappear. The Nazis - the ultimate magicians.

"We're reeling, John. The Pentagon, Homeland, Congress, probably even the White House itself can't be trusted. This had to be orchestrated with the blessing of those with the power to close down the country's defences. The National Guard are fighting, but the military, air force, navy? It's a shit show already, and the first strikes were only two hours ago."

The mercenary walked a fine line indeed. It was all true, but time was malleable here. History, outcomes, life, death, fate...everything was negotiable, wasn't it?

"Fuck," said Henry.

This game's in your head, but you're completely at its mercy, too, aren't you?

Must be hard, thought the mercenary. Depressing, really, when people discover they aren't the masters of destiny. They couldn't even control their own fate. The world spun out of any human's grasp. This world, and all worlds.

"New England was hit hard. If Boston's ablaze, though, New York's an *inferno*. Reports of millions dead, expected to rise by the minute and the strikes are still ongoing...we seem all but toothless to respond. There are even rumours that our own ships and planes have fired on us."

"My God."

"East coast, too. Every major city. All contact has been lost with San Diego and San Francisco. The *'Reich's'* fleet looks to be moving in force on Oregon in the North, the Baja California peninsula. Subs ranging down from the Andreanof Islands. Heavy artillery, and a small yield nuclear detonation reported in the Yukan territories. Two of our largest armoured divisions, and possibly 900 tanks, and the Alaskan front...*gone*. The north is open to a land invasion. We're tail in a Trans Am on Prom night, John."

"I can't believe it. They're invading *us*? The U.S.A.?"

The mercenary shook his head. "The USSR, too. Ranging in from China and Europe. Here, the might of the Nazi fleet and there, massive bombardment from the Asian front and land and armour assault from Poland to..."

"It's happening. It's the end."

*

Henry wasn't *genuinely* terrified, though.

When he said *'It's the end,'* he meant of the game...not of humanity.

This is FPS lore, right? It's not Civilisation or Total War. It isn't down to generals, or planning. This is twitch response and big guns and nothing more complex than counting up the bodies.

"We're facing the end of..."

Needs to be big, doesn't it? That's how stories work, how games work...they have to *escalate.*

"And?" said Henry, with a slight smile. "Guns, right? A beautiful woman with mad martial arts skills working for some kind of underground resistance? Meet her in the basement of the White House, fight our up, find out it's not the Secretary of Defence but the *gosh-darned President himself!* He's an impostor, though, right? Because the public won't buy into the actual President as a Nazi, will they? So you'll tone it down because the publishers won't agree to anything that'll lose sales. Right? I'm right, aren't I?"

"What?"

"Oh, come on. I'm tired. Where's the save point? I want a Coke and a sit down."

"John?"

"I'm Henry. *Henry.* Let me out. I don't know what this is...but *I don't want to play anymore.*"

"Are you?" said a voice he hardly remembered from a thin woman in her thirties. The woman walked like she was dancing toward Henry.

"What...what...?"

She was thin, pale, with long thick hair and bright, stunning, blue eyes. She wore a military uniform.

"...Sally? *Franziska?*"

"Lieutenant Grim, Mr. Severance. You have no rank, so you don't have to salute me. Civilian contractors are not beholden to me."

"Then I want out. This is...madness. I *know* you. I want out. And a Coke."

"But I'm perfectly happy to have you shot for a traitor."

"Forget the Coke."John, superbad-badass-bad-motherfucker, wanted to cry. He had one ally, and...she was just in his head, too?

Jarring, shaking, that earthquake wasn't in the graphics, or the physics, or any of the visible mechanics behind this insane world. The earthquake was real, and it was in his head, a blinding, terrible pain like a migraine, narrowing his vision so he could only see the woman before him.

Franziska. Sally.

He just didn't know.

"*Amy*? ...I need help," he whispered.

The woman, whoever she really was, marched him away from Dwayne Newell and from whatever tenuous hold on reality Henry Brandon had. Newell shrugged, as though they were best buddies. Like, *what can I do?*

Henry thought he might have more arrayed against him than this mysterious woman who seemed to appear whenever those mind-quakes happened, though. He thought perhaps the game itself was his enemy.

This is Silent Hill, now, where I find out I'm really dead, or in some netherworld. Any minute it'll be Pyramid head and confusingly attractive faceless nurses.

"*Amy*...?" he whispered again. "*Please.* Seriously."

She didn't reply.

He reached up to check his helmet with the arm not all twisted up by the woman who claimed to be Lieutenant Grim but could've been the GrimReaper herself.

All he found up there on his head was hair, but...

Something new.

A parting made by the burning furrow of a bullet from an SS trooper.

CHAPTER THIRTY-SIX

Poor bastard.

Franziska didn't like what she saw in Henry Brandon's eyes – he looked broken apart, like he might actually have had some kind of mental breakdown. And who could blame him?

"Get in the car," Sally told him.

When Henry was in the car, she turned her back on the closed door and Henry and levelled her military-issue sidearm at the mercenary's gut.

"Ms. Grim?" said the Merc. "What do you think you are doing?"

The pistol wasn't the Beretta M11 of Henry Brandon's world. In Henry's reality, the military didn't use German, like the SIG, or most European guns. In this reality, Franziska Grim looked the same, spoke the same, and used whatever got the damn job done. Now? ASIG Sauer P320, chambered with .40 Smith and Wesson rounds. It had more than enough punch to ruin the mercenary's constitution and take out his spine, too.

"You think you're the only one who saw this coming?" she said, her face suddenly fierce, and her mind on rails and her eyes as implacable as a runaway train. "This is *scripted*. You're essential...*so am I.I will* shoot you," she said.

Here, Franziska wasn't the woman who pretended to be mousy, who hid her light beneath her hair and avoided people. Here, she was the woman who hid away. The woman in whom a brilliant man had entrusted the future of mankind.

In this reality Franziska Grim was herself. The agent she'd trained most of her life to be. Freedom's last hope.

John Severance wasn't the only badass in the game.

"You can't kill me," said the Merc and laughed in her face – no humour, just spite. "I thought you were intelligent. You're not your father, are you?"

If the mercenary thought his words could sway her, he wasn't as good at reading people as he thought he was.

Franziska shrugged, but her eyes and the gun were steady.

"No. I can't kill you."

Three uniformed men approached as she flicked her hand toward them.

"They probably can't, either. You're *scripted*. You're end game, for sure, but who wins? When the credits roll, you really think they'll be in German? Fuck you. I might not be able to kill you. In fact, I'm sure I can't - *yet*. But I *can* have you limping into your next turn on the screen, right, *boss*?

"Gentlemen,' she said to the trio of serious looking marines she'd beckoned. "Escort this man from the base. Forcibly and violently if he resists. *Please.*"

"Sir," said one of the marines, and saluted.

She nodded.

"I'll see you soon," said the mercenary.

"You think you're the hero in this story?" she said.

"*Everyone* thinks they're the good guy," said the Merc. "That they're going to win, that they're the ones who'll be left standing. Nearly all of us have to be wrong."

He tipped an imaginary hat to her as the marines led him away.

CHAPTER THIRTY-SEVEN

Henry stared out the car window at the base. USAF airmen and women ran around like...

Like civilians.

Like men and women trained for war, and suddenly finding out they weren't fighting a war, but *losing* it.

"Henry? You OK?"

Franziska started the car. Slowly, a man asleep waking up, Henry turned away from his reverie.

"What did you...?"

"Henry. I called you Henry Brandon. I'm..."

Henry blinked, then stared at her this time. No shifting scenery. No jarring, no earthquake in his mind. He reached up. No combat helmet.

Unable, exactly, to think, Henry found there were flashes someplace at the edges of thought. Not mind-quakes, these. Lightning. Fast. Too slim to grasp.

"Sally...?"

"I'm no more Sally than you're John Severance. You're Henry, and my given name is Sauer. This is a VR world, an alternity, and you're losing yourself to it."

Henry frowned.

"I'm not losing myself. It's a game. I'm playing it. It's bugged, though, because I can't find a save point. I can't save. I can't..."

"Henry, stop. Stop. It's okay. There *isn't* a save point. Here, there - *no reloads.*"

That resonated.

"What? What did you say?"

"Henry, close your mouth for Christ's sake. You're about five seconds short of dribbling. Man up. Fuck. Quit being such a pussy."

"Sally...Franziska?"

"Well done."

Even five seconds from dribbling catatonia, that sarcastic tone got through to Henry. First Amy, now her. He felt like a school kid again, waiting for a teacher to bring him down. Like being married, his wife always put him down. Before that, his parents.

You'll never be good enough.

The subliminal message barely concealed beneath all their jibes.

"In 1998 my father left me a letter," said Franziska. "In it, he laid out my life...right up until the moment when I was supposed to meet *you*. From this moment...*now*...I have precisely no clue what's going on or what's going to happen. But I do know what's *real*."

Franziska spoke as she drove. She drove like she was angry with the car. She didn't slow for the gate. Going that speed, coming in, the guards on duty would've riddled the car with bullets. Out, no one cared. Nothing was on fire, and the car's plates told them all they needed to know. By the time she reached the gate, the barrier was up and the rising bollards which would've been deployed to stop a terrorist or attacker already retracted.

"Game or not, I don't know what comes next...that's just living, isn't it? Does it matter what you call it?"

Franziska laughed, and there was something wild about the laugh, just like the way she drove. "Henry, my father saw the ascendance of the Nazis. He saw the Reich rise triumphant and the *Kaiserreich*'s shadow. He foretold the fall of Europe and of most of Asia."

"Like a fortune teller?"

"Not like Nostradamus or like he saw it in a dream, or a crystal ball. With computers, with language, code...with science."

He watched her in the rearview mirror, then, leaned forward in his seat so he could see her without the filter - even a mirror was too much like looking at a replica at this point.

She smelled like a real person.

What do I smell like? Sweat, Nazi blood? Bad breath from cigars? Fear?

"You came to my house and I put on a VR headset. Did that happen?"

"Yes. Yes it did. And that man back there, he's as real as you or I, and perhaps more dangerous than the both of us."

"I don't feel dangerous. At this point I've been to Holland and to Macao. I've killed...good God...I set off a nuclear detonation? I don't even know now. If this is war, and I'm some kind of super soldier, then I'm a hero. If I'm delusional, I'm just a really successful murderer. If any of that's true, if any of what you say is true...doesn't make a difference. I'm fucking insane. And you sat in my spot on my couch. In my house. Did any of that happen? None of it?"

"All of it. Shut up, okay? I'm rude, I get it. But Henry, listen, please. You and I have to work together. The man we left behind works for the

Nazis. He's been around for decades, and he's in here with us, with the same rig..."

"So, it's not a single player game. So what? You're here..."

"Fuck, Henry...*listen*. When I came to you and made you put on the headset...a few minutes later, a mercenary came and he's got both of us hostage – our other bodies. But really? *There's no difference, Henry.* This *is* real...it's just a different kind of real. Game, virtual, alternate universe...it doesn't matter. It's all the same thing. What happens here affects what happens there. The game's not broken, Henry. You can't take it from your head even if you could. You're wired in, and taped down, and too weak to move if you weren't."

"Too weak?" said Henry.

"Henry, it's a portal. It's a doorway. The Nazis knew about it all along. Do you understand that? They know we're coming."

Henry shook his head.

"I'm not going anywhere. I'm already there. I'm insane. I had a stroke. A heart attack. I died and this is hell."

"Don't be a dick. The USSR will fall, we'll fall, and then? The entire world is gone. Everything, lost. Humanity as it could have been. History, progress, art, literature – anything the Nazis do not wish for will be expunged. People, races, languages. Ways of life. Evil reigns supreme. You think this is hell? This isn't hell. This is the last chance to close the door on hell, Henry. Our chance to *slam* that door."

"Like, we change the past?"

"*No.*" She puffed, reaching for patience. "You can't time travel, John...except to the future...you know how you send people to the future?"

"No?"

"They get older. That's it. You want to send something...you just leave it where it is. That's *history*, Henry. Time travel is just history. You can't break or bend time. But you *can* move sideways. This place affects our world. Maybe all worlds, all realities. Maybe my father knew that, maybe he didn't, but this is just as real as that burn on your scalp."

He reached up and felt it, and felt the pain of the burn across his head.

"My body and yours, with a rod in your back and your sticks...it's here. It's now. There's no going back unless we win."

At the mention of his sticks, of his back, Henry felt that jolt again. A jolt like...lightning...a shift, like standing on a fault line and the world jumps.

"You've been in this world for five days. The U.S.A. - as we know it - truly is under attack. That man, the one you thought was C.I.A.? He's a mercenary and he is not a figment of your imagination. He's part of the script but he's real, too. He exists. We exist, too, Henry, and because of that, your body...back there? It's dying...and so is mine."

Suddenly, Henry couldn't see her any longer. Could barely hear her. He'd been afraid before, but this was worse. His heart raced and it sounded as though she were speaking to him under water. .

"Sally...Franziska...my head hurts. This is all...quakes. Lightning...storms in my head."

He felt the car slow, but his vision was blackening, and the world, whatever world, fading.

No, he thought. *No...not know. Not a cut scene.*

He fought to hold on. He thought he still spoke. He thought he was pleading, maybe, trying to get through to whoever this woman really was. He didn't know. Maybe he was calling for his mother, or calling for Amy, or just pleading to whatever God there was who'd allow this fucked up facsimile of sanity come to pass.

He felt someone's fingers and hands holding his head, and something pushed into his ear.

Sound settled. His vision was strange. Franziska came back into view, but full of dots and wavering colours, like he'd rubbed his eyes too long and too hard. Fractal patterns, bursts of light dancing across his vision.

"This will help. Trust me."

Like a migraine...like being hit in the head, and drunk, and having a headache to start with. Like strobe lights and loud music and what an acid trip must feel...

Henry reeled and vomited into thefoot well in the back seat.

"Better?" she asked, and she didn't sound sarcastic or like she was laughing at him.

He panted, wiping his mouth, bile burning his lips and throat.

"You are Henry Brandon. This earpiece...it's like...a link to both places. It'll settle you. Like an anchor. Okay?"

He nodded. What choice did he have but to believe her?

'Hello, John,' said Amy in his ear.

CHAPTER THIRTY-EIGHT

Absecon Bay, US Waters.

On the captured Oscar-Class Russian submarine, the *Chelyabinsk*, under Absecon Bay, north of Atlantic City, New Jersey, a Nazi commander ordered the launch of a P-700 Granit cruise missile.

Only eighty miles from Philadelphia, at around 500 miles an hour, launch to impact would take around six minutes.

Interstate 95, New Jersey Turnpike, South of Philadelphia, Franziska Grim and Henry headed south, her driving like a maniac, and panicked, crazed, terrified Americans of every stripe drove here and there all around them.

Panic just as dangerous as a Granit cruise missile.

But not for Franziska and Henry. She was an angry driver, but like most other things she did, she was a great driver. Fast, too.

Even so, no one drives faster than a missile.

CHAPTER THIRTY-NINE

Big Timber Creek, New Jersey, USA

"Henry," said Franziska. "Calm down. Listen. It's okay. Everything is..."
Henry panted, panicked, hyperventilated...but...
'...okay.'
Amy's voice finished Franziska's sentence.
'I am an artificial intelligence, developing along with this reality...this reality isn't just coded, Henry...it was grown. It's a living thing. It doesn't eat...but it evolves...it has been doing so since my father laid the first lines down on a screen.'
"No...this is ridiculous. You're not..."
"Think, John. Listen, Henry. Listen to me..."
Was that Franziska? Amy? Sally?
"No," he said, replying to Amy.
Am I? Who am I speaking to?
'Listen to her...'
It wasn't like he listened, but this time, he *heard*. A passive thing, a child's building block clicking into place. Like the way a smell brings back a memory, or a snippet of a song sits somewhere low down in your mind.
"Your voice...her voice..."
The quakes, the flashing, strobing lights, the sense of lightning in his mind all disappeared and for the first time since donning the headset, Henry felt whole.
While Henry had been sick, Franziska had pulled the car to the side of the road. She started the engine again and pulled out into the flow of traffic.
"She's my thoughts, Henry...as they might have been."
"Like...sisters?"
"More. Like twins," said Franziska.
Henry shook his head. "This is..."

"Mental, right? Of course it is. And if Amy's my twin, maybe John Severance is yours."

Franziska and Amy's voice were becoming one. Stereo, saying the same thing, but into each ear. Slightly out of sync...and then...not. Perfect. Like everything coming together.

"That's..." *Nonsense,* he thought. But he wondered, too, if his voice was his, or John's, or if they were one and the same.

"You're the badass here," said Henry. "John Severance...me...whatever...Franziska? What do we do? What are we supposed to do?"

"Save the world, Henry."

He laughed. "Of course. Should I call you Franziska? Amy?"

"Franziska, I think. Henry, right?"

"Yes."

"With you here. Things feel different. Like..."

"Like something coming together?"

"Yes. Like that. Like your voice...Amy's voice...like you think and she speaks, or she thinks, you speak. Like stereo becoming mono. Franziska...if you and Amy feel closer..."

"Yeah."

He didn't need to say it. If that was happening, then maybe this game, this alternity, and *his* reality were getting closer, too. Two streams becoming one, like reality was thousands, billions of tributaries joining some vast river, something beyond imagining...one true sea of time into which everything flowed, and broke away again. People, thoughts, events, the vastness of human history and the world and the solar system, the galaxy - the universe, even - just drops of water in some ocean bigger than everything that was or could be.

Even so, reeling and confused as Henry was, Franziska's driving was terrifying.

"What now?"

"We get to Washington...then we kill the President of the United States before it's too late," said Franziska as the P-700 fired from the *Chelyabinsk* blew out the bridge over Big Timber Creek behind them.

Chunks of road, steel, car and people rained down. A shard of metal speared the trunk of their car, killing the fuel line, the fuel tank, and the right wheel, brake pads, springs, tyres.

On a really good run it's around seven hours from Hanscomb USAF base, MA to Washington, District of Columbia. It takes quite a while longer when your car explodes.

ACHIEVEMENTS:
Spy

WEAPONS UNLOCKED:
SIG Sauer P320
Capacity: 14 rounds. Ammunition: .40 Smith and Wesson.

PART FIVE

CAPITOL

'We now have direct confirmation of a disruptor in our midst, one who has acquired an almost messianic reputation in the minds of certain citizens. His figure is synonymous with the darkest urges of instinct, ignorance, and decay. Some of the worst excesses of the Black Mesa incident have been laid directly at his feet, and yet unsophisticated minds continue to imbue him with romantic power, giving him such labels as '*The One Free Man*', or '*The Opener of the Way*'. Let me remind all citizens of the dangers of magical thinking. We have scarcely begun to climb from the dark pit of the evolution of our species. Let us not slide backward into oblivion just as we have finally begun to see the light. If you see this so called free-man, report him. Civic deeds do not go unrewarded and likewise complicity with his cause will not go unpunished. Be wise. Be safe. Be aware.'

-

Half-Life 2
-Valve Corporation 2004

CHAPTER FORTY

New Jersey, NJ Turnpike

The wreckage of the bridge, along with the burning hulks of maybe fifty cars full of shattered bodies, was strewn across the landscape for hundreds of yards. Close up, it was the kind of destruction few ever truly see. They see the aftermath of explosions and death on the television. Detached, through a lens.

The epicentre of the blast was the bridge, but powerful enough that the waters of the creek vaporised, too. Smoke and steam filled the air.

Henry and Franziska's car had been reduced to shards of metal and burning rubber.

He crawled toward her. She, thrown clear when the car flipped and her door opened. He, through the windshield. Henry thought perhaps his arm was broken.

"Franziska?"

She didn't reply. There was a horrible tear in her forehead. He thought she was dead, but then she coughed and groaned, rolled over on the road and bled on him when he held her. No interlude. No cut scene. Just pain.

People cried out all around them. Real tears and anguish, real screams and terror.

He wanted to help the people dying and hurting all around them, but they had to help themselves to help others, didn't they?

Why does it worry me, leaving a bunch of game extras to their agony?

They didn't *feel* like game extras. They didn't *sound* like it. Those cries – hundreds of souls, maybe - didn't seem like something even Franziska's father could do. Nothing technology but bombs could achieve such perfect suffering.

He shifted to better see Franziska's wound and something dug into his stomach.

The emergency medical kit the nurse had given him.

He remembered what those syringes could do. He'd needed stitches, and in a matter of hours, he hadn't.

Henry pulled Franziska eyelids open. Her eyes jittered back and forth in their sockets, like she was following a game of Pong on speed.

"Franziska? Can you hear me?"

His arm hurt. Like Amy and Franziska were closer, like he and John were closer - maybe this world of Professor Sauer's imagining and brilliance and their world grew closer, too. Becoming *one*.

"Hold on," he told her. The blood from her forehead was pouring. Concussion, definitely. Brain damage? Maybe.

He took one syringe from the pack– how he still had it, he didn't know, or care– and stuck in into her arm. He didn't know how to find a vein but figured a serum that could heal a wound needing stitches was probably clever enough to get where it needed to go.

He only had one more. He thought he might regret using it up later, but a broken arm was a broken arm.

The serum from the last syringe moving into his own bloodstream, Henry held Franziska and waited. At that moment, with her in his arms and people dying around them, Henry Brandon discovered something about himself. Not about John Severance, but him. He *wanted* to kill Nazis. He wanted their drying blood daubed on his cheeks, in the cracks of his palms, beneath his fingernails.

His eyelids grew heavy, and he slipped into unconsciousness, he and Franziska in an untidy huddle, lost in drifting smoke.

*

The next time Henry opened his eyes, it was dark. There were no emergency vehicles. No one moved them, and bodies still littered the roadside. Everyone who could had fled, and everyone else was probably dead.

There were no civilian ambulances or handy Samaritans. It wasn't life as usual. It was war, and Henry was John Severance just as John Severance was Henry. He wasn't a potbellied gamer on a couch any longer.

He was a warrior.

Franziska was quiet. He shook her, gently, and wiped at her brow. The blood, dry, came away. Beneath was just a heavy, angry scar.

She opened her eyes.

"We're still alive?"

"Looks that way," he said. "And, Franziska?"

"Henry?"

"Let's make the bastard pay. All of 'em. Every single one of them. I won't close my eyes again. I promise you. Let's go knock some Nazi teeth in."

He stood, and pulled her to her feet.

"Do you know how to steal a car?" she asked.
"No," said Henry, "But I happen to know a guy."

CHAPTER FORTY-ONE

In the western states, the land invasion was well underway. The *Kaiserreich* came on in three heads, their advance a Hydra, those heads snapping at the U.S.A. From Baja, through Oregon, and down from the barren Alaskan wasteland in vehicles designed to handle fallout from the ballistic missiles which wiped whole armoured divisions from existence.

Seven thousand bombs hit US soil in the first thirty minutes. A storm of unimaginable, inconceivable ferocity, and the largest land force in the history of mankind drove in behind it. They came not for gold, or blood.

Along the Eastern seaboard the Nazis forged paths from Virginia, Delaware, and Maryland. A hundred thousand black-gloved fists working as one to grasp the Capitol of the United States of America and so crush the country to submission.

In the early days of this war, such a seemingly simple thing as advancing an army a few hundred miles would have taken months. Hard fought in trenches, town and forest, in deserts and hills and oceans, with tanks and militarised vehicles, paratroopers, submarines, dive bombers, and buckets of blood. Here? In this place?

The most successful empires didn't crush the enemy, but assimilated them. It didn't lessen its own numbers in battle, but grew with each victory, each culture and land and people it absorbed into its mass. Even without the *Luftwaffe*'s strength and command of the skies, the *Kaiserreich* wasn't just Germany. It was global. It was money, and corporations, and control, and when the *Kaiserreich* marched, it marched with an army close to eleven million strong at its back.

*

Once, Germany fought a war on two fronts, and Russia prevailed.

This time, as the last, Russia fared far worse than the US.

Russian resources, and thus Russia's value to the Reich, was not in populous areas but beneath the tundra in the bitter Siberian wastes. The cities did not matter.

From St. Petersburg to Vladivostok, a hundred million died. North to South, nearly three thousand miles of desolation. Cities dust after a blanket of ballistic missiles. In a matter of hours, Russia was reduced to a radioactive wasteland, it's people just dust drifting in the atmosphere.

Russia would never capitulate. The *'Reich'* knew that.

*

The USA would. It already had.

To defeat your enemy, people have to know it's a victory. You need annihilation to destroy an enemy, but if there's to be anything left to take, it's not annihilation but *capitulation* you need. Surrender. Not the army. Not the country.

You take the *head*. To get an entire country to bend its knee one must take the first knee.

People would fight back, of course, and for many years. There would be insurgents and insurrections, rebellions and riots...but they would be quelled. Expunged.

How long until only pockets of resistance remained, and then nothing but whispers in sewers and dark alleys, until, finally, silence?

But one person can *always* make a difference. Don't believe that?

Adolf Hitler did. He began it.

Perhaps it might take two to end it. Franziska Grim, and Henry Brandon.

CHAPTER FORTY-TWO

Deptford Township, Gloucester County
U.S.A.

The 12th Panzer Division, once infamous for surrendering to Russia in '45, this time received the honour of joining the invasion.

Henry and Franziska hid. The rumble of Panzer XV tank treads was a great incentive to practise your squats.

"We can't stay here forever," said Franziska in a hushed voice, entirely unnecessary against the background noise of an armoured division on the move. "I don't know how much time we have left."

"This isn't about time. It's revenge." The venom in his voice worried Henry, but he couldn't help his fury. "We lost. This is about killing as many as we can."

"If we can reach the military, get word out..."

"How? Satellites are down. Power grids are gone. The army is either fighting for the Nazis, hunkered down somewhere with lots of tinned food, or dead. *America* is dead, Franziska. Face it."

"Wars were fought before the microchip. How do we rally? One by one, if we have to. Should the President sign some accord handing us all over to *them*...that will the death knell. Until then, we fight. We...plan."

It sounded like nonsense to Henry, and he could see from her face she thought it was nonsense, too. She was drowning, floundering for anything to hold onto.

"We can't win. You see that. I know you do. There is no plan from here on out, is there?"

"No," she said, her voice quiet still, even though the last of the tanks were well past them. "But we have to do something. What we do here has to make a difference. It has to."

"Because your father told you so? In a letter? What if he was wrong?"

Franziska stared at Henry.

"No. Who remembers the characters in the stories we read, the games we play, the films we watch? We do, don't we? Didn't you ever wish you could be the one who stands up tall?"

He wanted to tell her no, but he didn't. He'd wished, sure he had. Maybe before a pot belly and divorce and a broken back. He'd wished for something more than life offered. He still did, he supposed - still wished he was the kind of man who reached deep down, and fought.

"Henry, just because we can't win, doesn't mean we shouldn't fight."

He wanted to tell her it didn't make sense...but he couldn't.

It was what humans did, and always would. *Fight.*

"Then what?"

"They want the head? We take it first."

*

The tanks rolled on north. Perhaps five hundred infantry, maybe thirty tanks. Probably tonnes of steel and whatever else could deflect shells and bullets worth millions. Maybe hundreds of millions. Hundreds of millions in Deutschmarks to destroy how many millions of people?

How much did it cost to end a life?

They watched the last of the 12th Panzer Division pass, rubble and tread tracks right through the centre of a town bereft of people.

Bereft. Where were the *people?*

"Henry...where are they? The people? We're not the only survivors, right? Should there be...someone?"

Henry nodded. "I've been thinking the same. It's like the game shows us only the important parts..."

"Henry..."

"Only what we need to see..."

"Henry," she said, and nudged him.

On the lot over from them, behind a chain link fence, was a car...sleek at the front, but with a heavy rear, like an arrow pushed along by a thoroughbred's hind legs.

"Jesus," she said.

Henry followed her gaze, and raised her. "Fuck. Is that a Bugatti Veyron?"

"What's a Bugatti Veyron?"

"Only one of the fastest cars ever made. In fact, the fastest road car. Something like 250 miles per hour."

"Who has one of these?" she said. "It looks like...like it goes fast."

"Fast?" he laughed. "It's ridiculously fast, and this...this is ridiculous. Hardly anyone has one of these," said Henry, glancing around at the lot.

Weeds. Run down. A few cars. Fires in the distance. No people. The fastest road car ever made in an abandoned lot. Right there waiting for them?

Franziska walked around the car.

"It doesn't say Bugatti, Henry. It says it's a 'Truffade Adder'."

"I never heard of one of those."

"I have," said Franziska. She shook her head and laughed. "Guess."

"What?"

"GTA."

"Get out."

"No. Get in."

"You drive. You're better at that than me."

Then, Henry muttered something to himself. It took Franziska a while to figure out what it was.

You couldn't hotwire one of these. She didn't have to. It was a simple push button. She pressed it and the thing roared into life, a monster ready to obey her commands.

They drove, both quiet, the engine loud, and Franziska figured out what it was Henry mumbled before they got in the car.

The game will provide, he'd said.

Like the car, the start button, was no surprise. He hadn't said a word.

She glanced at Henry. He stared out the window. Thinking.

She was thinking, too. Thinking maybe Henry had more of this reality figured out than her.

CHAPTER FORTY-THREE

New Jersey Turnpike –
295 through Wilmington -
195, through Delaware, Newark.

They drove some more. Each time they passed a car it was in one lane, or the other. Wrecks were at the sides of the Turnpike, then the Interstate...perfectly arranged so nothing got in their way.

Henry wondered, if he'd been able to see in the cars they passed at insane speeds, if there would even be drivers.

"Franziska...how long have we been...in this world...this...virtuality?"

"I don't know."

*

Maryland, through Baltimore –
Interstate 95

"How long do you think 'til our bodies die?"

"I don't know."

"Franziska."

"What?"

"You know you said about our bodies, dying in the real...other...*whatever* world?"

"Yeah?"

"And how things are getting closer...like you and Amy?"

"Yeah?"

"Franziska...I'm getting hungry. I don't feel like a badass...I feel weak."

*

The Adder never hit 250mph, but Franziska got pretty close.

130-odd miles until Washington DC. Normally, a journey of around two and a half hours. But on clear roads during an invasion? In a Veyron, or an Adder from GTA?

It wasn't normal. Nothing was normal. *Normal* wasn't normal.

*

"How old are you?"

"Thirty-eight."

"Really?"

"I was worried you were younger."

"Worried?"

"I was going to ask you out to dinner. Maybe a coffee. Probably a coffee. In the real world, I wouldn't. Here? I don't know. Here, it's like I'm wearing armour, but in my head. You know? I'm different here. Better."

"Better? Henry...you're not better. Different, sure. But you're a man doing the best you can...and that's good enough, isn't it? Not a superhero. My father saw a soldier playing your role, and by some accident, it fell to you. No training. A guy with a bad back and sticks and a moonshine computer. You stepped up. You - *Henry*."

Henry fell quiet.

*

Franziska drove well, and like a maniac. Nothing could stop them.

Nearly as fast as a missile, at last.

*

"How come you never married, Henry?"

"I did. We divorced."

"Why?"

"Didn't like each other anymore. I broke my back, went back to what I'd been...I played games. Escaped, I suppose. We forgot to speak to each other and kind of drifted. You?"

"Never married. Hard to get married when your father's seen the future and leaves you a letter detailing what you're going to be doing for the next couple of decades. And yes," added Franziska.

"Hmm?"

"I'd have said yes, I think. Probably. I understand what you mean about this place being like armour. But back there? In whatever reality? Yes. I'd have said yes."

"You're good enough, too, Franziska," he said.

*

It all went wrong as they hit the outskirts of Washington DC.

Gunfire stitched a row of spiders in the windshield and someone screamed. Henry realised it was him, a bullet to the shoulder, through and through.

Franziska twisted the wheel, not panicking, but trying to control a slide as she brought the Adder from 140mph to 50 in a matter of seconds. The ABS juddered, and the wheel fought her.

A tank rolled through a building beside them. A shell exploded behind them. A helicopter unloaded round upon round from heavy side mounted weapons.

"Fuck," said Henry as blood poured."Fuck, that hurts."

The tank stopped, and the Adder stopped. The turret turned toward them, and Franziska watched it in the remains of the shattered rear-view mirror.

"Hold on," she told Henry.

Then, she jammed her foot down and the car leaped forward, turning and accelerating as the tank fired. Bright fire filled the sky as the helicopter unleashed thousands of rounds a minute toward them, and nothing hit them.

A miracle, or design?

Writhing in agony, Henry honestly didn't give a shit.

The Adder's tyres squealed as they headed down, and down, and down, into an underground parking garage, where helicopters and tanks couldn't follow.

CHAPTER FORTY-FOUR

Washington DC

They tumbled from the car. Henry dripping blood. His arm thumped against his side as they ran.

On foot they were too slow. Unarmed,unarmored, they didn't stand a chance.

"Wait," said Henry, pale and more tired than he should be for a man who could probably pole vault, do the waltz and play the piano with his toes. "Tired. Go on. I'll rest a while."

"No, you won't, Henry," she told him as he leaned back against the stairwell wall and then slid down, leaving a bloody smear on his way to the floor. "You'll sit there, get cold, and your eyes will close, and then? Then you'll just drift away. Or a Nazi'll put you out of your misery."

She patted his belt. He wore different clothes, clothes he didn't remember changing into...like he'd been through some shift of perspective he'd missed, but the pack with the hypodermics was there on his belt.

"No time for that, Nurse Grim," he said, his smile weak. It seemed like the sort of thing John Severance would say. A bullet wound wouldn't bother *him*.

It's bothering me plenty, though.

His vision was coming and going, Franziska was wavering, and he was seriously thinking dying might be quite peaceful after all. Then she jammed the hypodermic right in his chest.

Henry bolted up, eyes wide. He missed breaking her nose with his forehead only because she was more nimble than a man with a shot of whatever *that* was. Adrenaline, euphoria, weightlessness...

"Man," he said. "Woo." He tore off the arm of his shirt, no harder right then than opening a bag of chips, and bound his wound, tying off the tourniquet with his teeth.

Franziska stared at him.

"Wow," she said. "That was, like, three seconds?"

"I feel great," he said, bouncing on the balls of his feet now. "What the hell was that? It's great. Brilliant. Wow. Brilliant."

"Don't know what it was, Henry," she told him. "But calm it, okay? Probably some battlefield drug. You're like a kid who just had a cocaine McFlurry."

"I feel..." *Invincible,* he thought, but didn't say it, because it sounded stupid. He certainly wasn't bulletproof.

"Or am I?"

"What?" said Franziska.

"Hmm?" said Henry, still bouncing.

Franziska shook her head. "Can I?"

He nodded and she took Henry's knife from his belt (*I missed you, buddy,* he thought. *Maybe I should give you a name. Bob. I'll call you Bob...*) then used it to hack at the concrete wall, loosing chips and dust, and scraped the dust together into one hand.

"Oh shit," she said. "There!"

She flicked her eyes, and Henry's eyes followed. Distracted, she pulled the tourniquet down and jammed concrete dust against the wound.

"Fuck!"

Then she pulled the tourniquet up again.

"There," she said. "Nurse Grim to the rescue. All done."

"The fuck?" Henry said, his high seriously dampened.

"What? You want a lollipop? Big baby. It'll congeal, slow the bleeding. It's a big hole, and I haven't got anything better. Come on. You can't die yet. Looks like it's a co-op game and if you wuss out I won't play with you again."

"Promise?" he said, but he laughed. "Good trick - *shit, there!* Got a plan?"

"No," she said. "I've been following the walkthrough for so long, I forgot this. This not knowing... It's kind of fun."

"Fun for who?" he said. "I got shot. Twice."

"Well, you should know better then. If it hurts, stop getting shot."

"What...I..."

"Shit," she said. "There. Hear that?"

"Nu-uh," he said. "What next? Impromptu dentistry?"

Not this time, though. Footsteps, higher up, headed down toward them. Heavy steps. Like combat boots. Of course they would be – it wasn't like there were any shoppers around.

They could run, sure. But for how long? To what end? You can't run forever. Doesn't matter if it's a game, or real life.

They nodded in unison.

Henry waited in view, and Franziska flattened herself against the wall. The first soldier would see Henry, lift his weapon...

For once, it came together just right.

The first Nazi came at Henry, when Franziska dropped, yanked, twisted, pulled the trigger on the man's rifle. The two men behind the point man fell.

Henry flipped his knife through the air, and it thudded into the man's eye, and brain. *Massive, catastrophic damage, instant brain death.* The perfect throw.

With his left hand, too.

Of course it was, he thought. *I can dual-wield heavy pistols. I'm ambidextrous, aren't I? Got that achievement. Skill tree'd that one right the way to the top. Next week, the circus?*

One man still lived. Franziska kicked him in the throat, and then he didn't.

Henry didn't blink or look away.

Nazis were just zombies, invading aliens, *fodder.* They weren't *human*, and he didn't feel bad at all.

Franziska pulled Henry's knife from a ruined eye socket, wiped it clean on the uniform and flipped it back. Henry caught it easily and slid it back in his sheath.

Ah, Bob. Welcome back.

He raised his eyebrows at Franziska, though.

"Don't stint on the weapons," he said. "Cough 'em up."

She sighed, took a SIG MG 710-3 for each of them. Nearly 10kg a piece, she handled them easily enough. Franziska handed one over to Henry, and he grinned.

"Don't get too frisky," she said. "Good weapon, but 50 rounds a piece. Don't waste them, Space Cowboy."

She relieved the corpses of pistols, too, and expertly checked the chamber and magazine on every weapon. All knock-offs of the ubiquitous Browning 1911 model, all effective enough, all fully loaded.

I should really remember how to do that, he thought. He didn't want to be caught with an empty gun. He'd need the ammunition, and soon. Boss level coming up. Had to be.

In Washington, all the way to The White House?

Boss level. No doubt.

"Zombies, Nazis, all the same, right?" said Franziska.

Henry nodded as they stepped over the pile of dead Nazis.

"Let's kill 'em all."

ACHIEVEMENTS:
Crash Test Dummy
Bullet Magnet
Drug Mule
Circus Freak
Buff Historian

WEAPONS UNLOCKED:
SIG MG 710-33
Capacity: 50 round belt-fed mag. 7.62x51mm Round. MaxRPM: 950

VEHICLES UNLOCKED:
Truffade Adder/Bugatti Veyron

TROPHIES:
Bob

PART SIX

LIKE A BOSS

The last thing that's gonna go through your mind before you die... is my size-13 boot!

-

Duke Nukem3D
– 3D realms 1996

CHAPTER FORTY-FIVE

Maryland Avenue –
Constitution Avenue –
Pennsylvania Avenue

Two matching black-and-red Ducati Diavels roared straight past the United States Capitol. The lights were off, nobody home. Henry suspected it'd been pretty much the same before the invasion.

North of National Mall on Constitution Avenue, then, north west to Pennsylvania Avenue. The Capitol Building, National Archives, the Old Post Office, all fell away in a blur as the heavy bikes hurtled Henry and Franziska toward the end of the game, the war, and maybe their lives.

They stole the motorbikes, of course - but not exactly, because they were there for the taking. They didn't have to kill anyone for them.

The ride was exhilarating. They needed no helmets– crash or combat helmet. Wind blasted their hair back, but there were no flies to swallow or dust in their eyes, because the game was coming together, wasn't it?

Henry didn't even need a HUD, or Amy. He had a Franziska. She was way better. She, if nothing else, was real.

The game was a portal, sure. A place wedged between a thousand, maybe a million, possibilities. There, in every other world, life was life, though – a constant battle between order and chaos. This place had evolved beyond mere life but in this alternate place, Henry understood one thing with no doubt at all: *there were still rules.*

Real life was a crap shoot, and you didn't get to choose whether or not you were born. Life could afford to be a dick. A game had to give you choices...it had to give you chances...or else, why play? Who plays to *lose?*

I used to play to lose, thought Henry as he and Franziska halted their bikes on the South Lawn, facing the grand old landmark. *Not anymore. Now I'm all in.*

*

Maybe a thousand soldiers were arrayed against them. Infantry. Sponges to soak up the majority of their ammunition, weren't they?

The seasoned fighters would come after...the *SS*. And by then, Henry and Franziska would be low on ammo. This was the finale, wasn't it? It was *supposed* to be harder. Supposed to be the ultimate challenge, the test of a gamer's metal.

But a lesson Henry learned when he was a mere nipper, playing Resident Evil, was to hold *something* back. Back then, how many times had he wished he'd saved some bullets, or shells, or some god-damn thing? Too many. It was a hard lesson he'd learned slow no matter how many times some mutant behemoth crushed him and the ridiculous spanner that was his only remaining weapon.

"Henry," said Franziska. Both were still astride their motorcycles. "You look kind of smug. It's weird. Stop it."

"Just thinking," he said.

"Want to share?"

"Sure," he said. "Coffee?"

"Seriously? We're about to die and you're going to hold me ransom for a coffee?"

"Well...I really would like to go for that coffee. What you gonna do?" His smile was infectious.

"Deal," she said. "So? What gives?"

"What do you think? Exposition first, or after this bit? A two-part battle? Three?"

"What?" she said.

"How long have you been playing games, Franziska?"

"A long time. Why?"

"Because you enjoy games?"

"I don't know. Sometimes? My father told me it was important. Like guns, fighting..."

"Like studying?"

"I suppose. Theory, level design...yes. Study. I guess." She shrugged.

"I play, Franziska. You know the best way to learn something? Enjoy it. It's far easier to learn something you enjoy than something you don't. You haven't noticed a fair bit, and I've been thinking, so...yes. I'm smug. Not 100%, because this thing, this...alternity? It's not like any game I've played...but it *is*, too. It took me a while, because it's like realising a story in a book is the same as a story in a weekly TV show, or in a game...there are *rules*. We don't know all of them, and sometimes they change...but there are lines of script and hints along the way if your eyes and ears are working fine. Mine weren't. Now I think they are."

"You're making no sense."

"Welcome to insanity, then, Franziska. I've been in this here asylum since the first time I put that set on. Think about this - why haven't they opened fire? We're just sitting here. They could hit us with their eyes shut. A thousand or so soldiers, firing in our general direction right now?"

"They're...not trying?"

"Exactly. Because this isn't the boss battle. It's like a prologue to a story within a story, and it needs explanation...basically, we could sit here talking and until we stop...the game's on hold."

"Can we just go home?"

"No...if someone were playing us, they'd skip, go straight to the battle. But we're playing us and we can't pause ourselves...the game does it for us," said Henry. "Look."

Around the edges of the South Lawn, three previous attacks had been stopped. Not tanks, but military vehicles riddled with holes from large calibre guns. Some small fires still burned, and a few bodies were sprawled on the perfect grass inside black railings smashed under the trucks and APVs. Spread out, though. Like you could run from one discarded prize to the next.

Henry was willing to bet there would be crates, too. Probably stashes of grenades, guns, magazines, maybe even an RPG with some long, unwieldy and unnecessary name like an Mk 153 Shoulder-Launched Multipurpose Assault Weapon. Or something like that.

The game provides what's needed, when it's needed.

In survival horror, you stockpile ammo for the big moments. Like in Resident Evil, a lesson learned through innumerable game-deaths. But in a shooter, it wasn't about being frugal. It was a *shooter*. It was about bullets, and guns, and bits flying off inhuman enemies, like zombies. Like Nazis.

If you're going to kill endless Nazis, you've got to have enough ammo for it to be fun.

He explained this to Franziska, and she wasn't slow.

"Okay, Henry," said Franziska. "So it's the boss battle, right?"

"I think so."

"Me too. Makes sense, because while you've been prattling on about how clever you are, I've been looking up there at the roof of the White House. You know, where that insanely huge gun is?"

CHAPTER FORTY-SIX

South Lawn
White House

Henry hadn't seen it because he hadn't expected it. It was night, so the air above the White House was dark and Washington DC was mostly without power – the Nazi strikes saw to that.

He couldn't understand how he could have missed it. Black metal, strange protuberances, indefinable shapes. A Transformer, a Decepticon, but one made from metal Lego bricks by an insane megalomaniacal monkey on acid. An evil obscenity straddling the White House with the largest gun ever built standing proud toward the sky.

The SS troopers who had held his attention seemed no more significant than flies on arhinoceros next to the gun.

In the distance, dwarfed by the White House and microscopic beneath that doomsday weapon, was The President of the United States. He walked toward them, a Nazi emblem on his lapel, his cadre of Secret Service behind him, in *SS* uniforms. News crews followed behind, and at either side, at a respectful distance. Respectful of the office, perhaps. Perhaps the man, too - doing nothing in the face of evil was always easy, but there would always be those who willingly threw in with the darkness, because it was where their hearts felt at home.

Above everything, the horrible, gargantuan gun looked down through the bore of a barrel the length of three Greyhound buses.

It was overkill. Of course it was.

The President halted in front of them.

"Mr. Severance. Very well done. I could have done it, of course, and better than anyone else could have done it. If I had wanted to do. I would be a great spy. Trust me."

Henry wasn't expecting that. "What?"

"Delivering Franziska Sauer to us. America's most dangerous enemy. Public enemy number one. An achievement. Congratulations. Your service to your nation will go down in history..."

Franziska listened to the blatant lies, mouth open.

She's actually gawping, thought Henry. She might have been worried...but he wasn't.

This is Bioshock. This is the twist, where the President himself tells me I've been a plant all along, or a cyborg, or...whatever.

Henry didn't listen to the rest. This was a part he could skip, so he did. He shot Potus in the head and the bullet killed both the President and his wig.

CHAPTER FORTY-SEVEN

The barrel of the gigantic gun lording over the White House whirred toward them, its mechanism as loud as a passenger jet coming in to land.

Franziska and Henry were linked, now. They knew what they had to do, and didn't need any more words.

Who else could it be, controlling that insane gun? The mercenary, and he had to die.

*

Franziska went left, Henry went right, their Ducati's spraying dirt and clods of grass high into the air.

The shell from the doomsday gun blew out most of the south lawn, half of the *Kaiserreich*'s own force, the *SS-SS*, the media, and around fifteen feet of dirt below, too. A cloud of soil filled the air.

Maybe that was the moment the game and the world meshed. Maybe it was the moment they both broke. Maybe it did both, or both were the same thing. History, reality, the possible and the impossible all became one.

*

It wasn't a plasma, or pulse, or fragmentation grenade which took the bike from beneath Franziska, but a *Stielhandgranate...*a stick grenade. Like it was 1940, still.

Franziska groaned, rolled to the only cover available - a headstone. Like a headstone would be on the White House lawn.

Sailor Boy.

Teddy Roosevelt's dog.

Here, a man in a tin Nazi helmet, a M1935 design, from the '40s. There, two Nazis in ceramic polymer combat armour rode a motorbike and sidecar. The man in the sidecar fired what looked to be a MP35, favoured weapon of the Waffen-SS, with its distinctive side-mounted magazine.

What in fuck?

Franziska ducked her head back behind the headstone. That stone, it was incongruous, impossible...but there because it was *essential*. The game wasn't just giving them a boss fight, but fighting chance, too. To do so, the whole world was glitching, confusing itself. Breaking and mending.

Henry's ideas, about rules, about structure, about *lore*, was making more and more sense to Franziska, but a theory didn't stop bullets, did it?

She unslung her SIG MG 710-33 from her back and returned fire. The motorcycle and sidecar spun into the air, exploding, the riders thrown impossibly high. A Nazi ran from behind a tree which hadn't been there a moment before. She stood and shot from the hip.

Another Nazi missed. She didn't.

She ducked back behind Sailor Boy's tombstone, and three sniper shots send chips of marble flying past her face.

Fair enough, she thought, breathless but unafraid. *No one likes a camper.*

Franziska broke cover and ran.

*

Henry saw her go down, yelled out. He saw her get up again, take fire and return fire.

He had his own problems.

It was a blast from a tank that took Henry's Ducati from under him. The shell cratered the ground and the bike couldn't handle the dip. He tumbled away, rolled and grunted, winded.

He should run to Franziska, but he was tired, bleeding, disoriented...and when that big gun powered up again? Then they were both dead, and the *Kaiserreich* won.

Like The House of the Dead, as long as one of them went on, they had a chance to end this.

The mercenary wasn't the Nazi empire itself, was he? But you couldn't fight the entire might of the Kaiserreich in an FPS. Evil needed a face, just like perfume ads need a celebrity. People need something solid to rail against.

SHODAN. Alma. Kerrigan.

Evil needs something to *hit*, otherwise, it's all just prancing around in a VR headset trying to punch the sky.

Henry pushed himself to his feet and saw a bright light above the White House. Blue light, like electricity, coruscating up the sides of the White House toward the mega-gun.

Every boss fight he'd ever had, the boss had had some kind of tell - a weakness. Sometimes it was obvious. Mostly, frustrating, and he looked up a walkthrough. Here, everything he'd learned in nearly four decades of playing games was his walkthrough. That blue, crackling electricity meant the big gun was powering up again.

Run? Hide?

Nobody can outrun a bullet, or a missile, or a shell, and Henry or John Severance couldn't outrun electricity...but...

Henry looked around, and saw a tank circling his position. Almost like it was meant to. Like going in a wide circle was its only job in this whole mad world. He smiled.

Moving cover.

CHAPTER FORTY-EIGHT

Real life was a great poker player. This world, he figured if he learned its tells, he and Franziska might just be able to bluff their way to winning the entire pot.

The blue fire became painfully bright. The barrel of the mega-gun turned toward him, while Franziska's machine gun blazed in the night somewhere to his right. He ran to the tank, hard as he could, no chance to fire, or dodge. If he got hit, he was done. He slid, ducked, closed his eyes.

He heard the blast - lightning, thunder, a backfire, the 4th of July in Texas rolled into one.

The burning tank flew overhead, and Henry was still alive.

*

Franziska ran toward a doorway. Henry was out there, somewhere, fighting for his life. One of them had to win. She had no choice but to leave him and hope he made it.

She kicked in a French Door and rolled into an opulent state room in the White House, somehow beautiful, somehow sordid. On a desk was a combat jacket – like a flak jacket.

Power up, she thought, and strapped the jacket on.

*

Henry ran - sort of ahead, sort of to the side. *Strafing*. W and D at the same time, so he could keep that big cannon in sight and move toward the White House.

Inside, he found a loaf of bread and a bottle of ale on a table.

Like an old Wolfenstein. Like red wine on an officer's desk, and maybe Wagner playing on a gramophone while he ducked and reloaded. He ate some of the bread and drank some of the ale, and found his strength and wind returning.

Then, ahead, he came to a door at the end of a long corridor which he couldn't open, and what must have been an endless stream of Nazis ran straight at him from the opposite end of the corridor. They were terrible shots, and their AI sucked, and Henry was cold-hearted with two steady hands. He only had to reload once, and when he was done the hall was littered with bodies and Henry didn't feel anything but happiness at the sight.

*

Franziska opened the door behind him, and Henry swung round, fired, and nearly took her head off.

She raised her eyebrows. In the room behind her, there were two bullet holes in the wall.

Otherwise, the room was stark. A table, a writing desk, a rug over parquet flooring, and a long row of windows.

"You can hit a thousand Nazis...I'm not sure you could hit me," she said. "Mechanics, right? Law and lore."

Henry nodded. "I think so," he said, and like he'd seen Franziska do, he checked his ammunition.

"Not bad," she said, with an approving nod.

"I *have* been paying attention, you know."

There were no more soldiers rushing them, but with the deafening, roaring noise of power and the movement of the mega-gun above them, theywouldn't have heard enemies approach anyway. In the lull, they stared at each other, both, perhaps, thinking the same thing. It was Franziska who voiced their thoughts.

"It's a co-op, right? We're supposed to work *together*."

"And we haven't been. I know. Our strengths against his weakness?" said Henry.

"The White House is basically a mansion. So...what do you find in a mansion?"

"Puzzles and clues," said Henry, completely sure.

"Yahtzee," said Franziska, mimicking Harley Quinn in a way Henry found rather affecting. He coughed.

She smiled, and pointed to a clear plastic holder on a nearby table holding pamphlets, guidebooks. She took a detailed map of all tourist areas of the White House.

"See?" she said. "I've been paying attention, too."

Both craned their heads down to study the map. Neither *saw* the mercenary's swift descent from the mega-gun to the south lawn. Bright flaming jets slowed his descent, but even jets couldn't entirely control the suit he wore. It weighed nearly 500 kilos, and with it, the mercenary was over 12-feet tall. A monster made of steel, aluminium and titanium alloys, palladium and silicon and copper inside, with a shit-ton of lead in weapons in every conceivable space on the suit. At 12-feet high and 500 kilos in weight, they *heard* him very well.

It was that split second that saved them. The mercenary, looking like a Starcraft Goliath, opened up with twin shoulder cannons. They were already in the corridor, running, ducking, and then sliding to get away from the nameless mercenary's fury.

CHAPTER FORTY-NINE

Maybe two thousand rounds per minute, maybe twice that, or four times...there was no way to tell how many rounds tore through the room, and the corridor behind it, and the room behind that. Forensics experts would've retired before trying to recover that many bullets. If he'd fired long enough, the Merc could have carved out a hole from one side of the White House to the other.

The suit he wore, melded with the metal and circuitry and augmentations in his body, moved exactly as a human body would move – with no more than a thought.

Man and machine strode through smoke and fire, his vision and the suit's sensors searching through all spectrums. He found nothing, and no one.

*

Franziska thought perhaps the noise of the Merc's twin cannons had broken her eardrums.

"He can't shoot us both at once if we split up, right?"

Henry was out of breath, winded. He shouldn't be, because it was a game. But it wasn't, was it? Not exactly...and it was *breaking*.

"We'll try," said Henry. "But whatever we do...the game's breaking."

"I noticed, too. Inconsistencies. Oddities. Like...1940's soldiers and..."

Henry remembered, what seemed like years ago, a Stuka flying over Rotterdam.

"It's..."

He was going to say mental, perhaps something more colourful, but didn't get the chance. The Goliath smashed through the wall and levelled both cannons at them. The mercenary grinned down, entirely encased in the suit – *one* with the suit. Only his face was visible through some kind of high-tech glass. Readouts and figures, graphs, perhaps showing the power of the suit or the state of the Nikkei index. Wires ran straight from the mercenary's skull - from his ears, his jaw, and even through his right eye.

He raised one boot and smashed it down, trying to crush one or the other of them.

They rolled, but the boot flattened Franziska's SIG MG, made it just scrap half-pushed through carpet and into concrete below that.

"Just stay there," said the mercenary. "You can't win. I get paid either way. You know why that is?"

One shoulder cannon turned Franziska's way. The other turned toward Henry.

"Because I work for *myself*."

Henry saw madness in the mercenary's every action, then, and understood. Something in the man ran even deeper than the augmentations Henry saw inside what should have been an eye. It was pure evil. That was the payment, wasn't it? Satisfaction of a job well done, and his job, his passion - everything which drove the man in the Goliath suit - was *death*.

Henry had only an instant to decide.

"Left and right," Henry thought to Franziska. "Trust me."

Play it, he thought. He willed her to hear him. *Play, Franziska. Play him.*

He dove away from the gun, ducking and running like crazy, using every part of John Severance's strength and speed and every part of his own blind hope that he would be quick enough, that Franziska would trust him, even if she didn't hear him.

"No!" Franziska screamed. "No! I don't want to die!"

Henry heard her words. Maybe luck, maybe hope, telepathy...whatever it was, this was the part where they won or lost. In the next thirty seconds.

*

"Ms. Grim," said the mercenary. "I'm so glad you made it this far. Perhaps with your last breath you can read out the credits for me. Your German is impeccable."

"You'll die. Maybe I can't kill you," she said, and forced herself to her feet, and to look evil in the eye. "But you'll die."

"I already have." The whole machine shrugged, twin cannons, too. "But I deplore long speeches..."

Both cannons swivelled down, and the multiple barrels began to spin.

Franziska gave him the finger, and Henry slid beneath, and between the Goliath's legs.

He fired straight up.

One shot.

The bullet from the German *Mauser HSc* travelled straight up, from groin to the tip of the mercenary's head.

There's always a chink in the armour. That's how games work, how stories work, and they're both just the same thing, aren't they?

CHAPTER FIFTY

The Goliath suit fizzed, crackled, and with a hiss of escaping air, the face plate opened.

"Who are you?" asked Franziska, a pistol in her hand and execution in her heart.

The mercenary stared back at her with eyes barely human.

He's already dying.

Then, something – like the voice of an enemy HUD, heavily accented, female, chimed in.

'I am E.V.A. - Enhanced Vindicator Armour, Mk.VII.'

"Eva?" said Franziska, standing over the dying suit and man. "Like Eva Braun, Eva."

'Yes," said the voice in a parody of pleasant surprise. "I shielded him at the moment of his death. I have protected his mind ever since. I am the artificial remnant which prolongs and enhances my lover. We continue the greater work, *nein*? His...soul. His soul rests in...me. *Er ist ein guter seele.'*

"Hitler?" said Henry. "Hitler. *The* Hitler. Hitler Hitler?"

"Meine Leibe...Adolf. *Ja.* Yes," said Eva.

"I shot Mecha-Hitler in the nuts?" said Henry.

Franziska's mouth was still wide open in shock when Mecha-Hitler, and E.V.A. had the last word.

The Goliath's left cannon fired, just once. Like a death burp, nothing more. A single round only, but it was enough to kill Henry Brandon.

"Die," said Franziska, and pulled the trigger. "Die," she said, and each time, nine times, she punctuated the word with a bullet.

CHAPTER FIFTY-ONE

Mecha-Hitler and his artificial body, EVA, were just cooling blood and burned-out circuitry.

Henry was dying, too, and he knew it. There were no reloads. He figured that was just, and right, too.

Death, he thought, *is the save point and the end credits rolled into one.*

At least the credits won't be in German.

Franziska held Henry's hand. He wished he could feel it, but his arms were turning numb as Death crept over him.

"What do I look like, Franziska? I've never seen...I wondered..."

Franziska smiled, and laid her free hand on his cheek.

"Like a hero," she said.

He smiled back. He didn't even think of looking at the wound in his chest. He'd rather see her eyes one last time. Stunning, blue, and this time shining with tears.

"I'm done, aren't I?" he said. "Doesn't look like I'm going to make that coffee. Shame...I liked you."

"Let's just skip to the end then," she said.

His last breath was on her lips.

CHAPTER FIFTY-TWO

Franziska stood on the ruined south lawn of the White House, watching as the 'choppers came in low, then landed atop the littered bodies of hundreds of dead Nazis.

She sniffed, and wiped her eyes, then folded her arms as men and women in crisp, important uniforms strode toward her. One, an iron-haired man with a straight back, stepped up to Franziska and offered his hand.

"Ms. Grim," said the Chairman of the Joint Chiefs of Staff.

She nodded.

"The President?"

"I think you just set your down helicopter on him," she said. She was covered in grim and blood, she ached inside and outside. She didn't have the patience for pleasantries or questions.

He took that in his stride, and showed no emotion at all. "The enemy?"

"Mecha-Hitler? Yes. Nothing but scrap."

"Thank you, Ms. Grim, for your service to your country. We're on the offensive, thanks to you and your partner. Russia and the US are fighting back, on both fronts. We will win."

I don't know if I care, she thought. She was tired of it all. Killing, fighting, following a game plan, winging it...whatever she did, whatever they did, did anyone ever really *win*?

"The President?" she asked. "A fake?"

"No," said the Chairman with a shake of his head. "Just a Nazi. Good shooting, ma'am. On both counts. The world won't miss the Nazis. This is the day the world turns, Ms. Grim. Thanks to you, and Henry Brandon. Ms. Grim...Mr. Brandon?"

She didn't register the name the Chairman used, not right away. "Henry's body is in there."

"God...such a shame. He'll get a state funeral. He's an American hero. Both of you."

"I don't want a state funeral," she said. "I want cocoa."

So much for heroes, she thought, but as she walked away from the Chairman, she registered the false note, the *glitch*. Franziska stopped.

"Wait...Chairman? Sir?"

"Ms. Grim?"

"Did you say Henry?"

"Yes, ma'am. Yes, I did."

She nodded, and this time, she didn't look back.

ACHIEVEMENTS:
Heroic Death
Nut Shot
Mecha-Hitler EVA-Killer

Special Achievements:
JUDGE DEATH: I AM THE LORE.

EQUIPMENT UNLOCKED:
M1935 Stahlhelm

WEAPONS UNLOCKED:
MP35
Capacity (Max): 32 Rounds. Ammunition: 9x19mm Luger Parabellum.
Max RPM: 540
Stielhandgranate

VEHICLES UNLOCKED:
Ducati Diavel

FINAL SCORE:
CANNON FODDER: 2,000,000
PLAYER CHARACTER DEATHS:1
TOTAL: 1,999,999
LEADERBOARD: #1: GrimReaper
#2: HenryBrandonRocks73

PART SEVEN
SAVE POINT

'They say they saved me, but I'm not sure saved is the right word.'
-
Deus Ex: Human Revolution
Eidos Montréal/Square Enix/2011

EPILOGUE

"Henry? Henry? You did it. Open your eyes, Henry. Open your eyes."

Henry groaned. Everything hurt...or...

Wait. No it doesn't. I got shot, didn't I?

His eyelids were sticky. He forced them open, and saw a fuzzy, blurred man.

"You changed history's course, Mr. Brandon...*und* saved my daughter's life. My faith in you... I am forever grateful."

The blurred man's accent was thick, very German, and his English clearly strained to the limits of his capabilities.

"I...I *died*." Henry thought to reply in German, but for some reason found he could not. He searched his memory, his mind, but the language simply was not there...if it ever had been.

"After the fashion, ja. I suppose," said the man, and Henry realised it wasn't his vision which blurred, but the *man*.

Henry was on a bed, propped up on lots of pillows, with wires and pipes, catheters, cannulas, bags dripping various fluids straight into his body. He felt with that much effort going into saving his life, he had to be real. The man with the heavy accent, though...

"Who are you? Are you...a *hologram*?"

The man nodded. "Ask the question you have the answer to, Mr. Brandon. Please. You are free to. Ask," said the brilliant man - a savant, a genius without peer – who still frowned when searching for polite words and structure in a language he had never mastered. "Free to ask."

"Are you...Dr. Sauer?"

Dr. Sauer's image, a projection, or a ghost, smiled warmly.

"Indeed, Henry. Very well done."

Henry took the praise, but he didn't feel particularly smart. He felt like a seal, taking praise for begging for a fish.

"You're dead. Am *I*? Am I dead? Am I *me*?"

"Henry Brandon, Henry. Does not matter at all, ja? Real is now. Here. Nothing more." Herr Professor Sauer shrugged.

Henry felt the answer lacked a certain clarity, just like the hologram.

"Henry. Here. Take a look," said the projection, and passed Henry a mirror.

Henry didn't question how a hologram could hold, or move a mirror, any more than he questioned how it could think, and react, and speak. Henry's questions didn't seem to have answers...and maybe the professor was right - maybe they didn't matter in the slightest.

It's my face, he thought, staring at his reflection, touching his skin. *But it feels...better. Healthy. My hair's different...my teeth...*

He chomped, testing them out, watching his jaw move, now broad with muscles he didn't remember having.

As though his muscles had been regenerated and...

"The bullet?" he asked.

"Gone, Henry. Marvellous, nein? This place has many secrets."

"Like you?"

"I am no secret," said Sauer, with a smile untinged by motive, but the professor's pain was clear enough in his eyes. "*You* know."

Ghost or projection, Sauer's sadness was real as anything Henry had ever seen.

"You can stand, should you wish. You suffer no longer damage."

Henry had gotten so used to walking without thinking about the pain, he didn't think to look for his sticks, or wait for that shocking twinge from the rod in his back, or his breath, wheezing...or...

It was only when he stood and that old fear surfaced, that something would spasm, that he realised all that was simply...gone.

It wasn't just a bullet wound that should have killed him. He was better than saved. He was *healed.*

He looked down at his feet, beneath his hospital gown. The feet were a good, healthy colour. His calves well-muscled. The gown was short, and he could see his forearms. He looked as though he could crush sledgehammers with the muscles there, and his huge, strong fists.

"Doctor...what is this?"

"No reloads...but second chance? Sometimes they come, ja? Ja. Second chances."

This time, Sauer's smile was pure warmth.

"Second chance is worth grabbing out," Sauer made the motion, "with both hands."

"I don't know what to say. I don't know what this is...real...virtual...alternate..."

"Like father says, Henry...does it matter?" said Franziska.

She stood in the doorway to the hospital room, her arms crossed, her bold eyes assessing Henry in a way that made Henry uncomfortable, but only because she looked at him like that with her father in the room.

Otherwise...that look made him far, far happier even than the fact he wasn't dead.

"Whatever it is we made, the Nazis are gone. We won. Game or not...we *won*."

"Did we?" he asked.

Herr Professor Sauer watched the two, a faint smile flickering along with his whole body.

"Yes. You and I. We won."

"Am I?" he asked. "We beat evil, but Franziska...I don't know who I am anymore."

"Who do you want to be, Henry?" she asked. "Maybe you can be *anything* you want...but not *whomever* you want. We are who we are, aren't we?"

"Yes," he said. "We are who we're meant to be."

"And *where* we're meant to be, too?" she said.

"Yes," he said, returning her gaze, and seeing nothing else at all.

Dr. Sauer smiled, glancing from one to the other.

"Lovely," he said. "This is very pleasant."

"Father," she said, blinking and looking away from Henry. "Don't you have somewhere you're meant to be?"

"No...oh. Ja," he said, glancing at a watch he didn't wear. "How peculiar. Ja. I do."

The hologram flickered, and faded away.

Franziska moved to Henry's side, and wherever, whatever, whoever they were, it was just right.

The End

www.ingramcontent.com/pod-product-compliance
Lightning Source LLC
Chambersburg PA
CBHW051951170626
46808CB00007B/2565